Penguin Books

The Glassy Sea

Marian Engel was born in Toronto and grew up in
various Ontario towns. She attended McMaster and
McGill Universities. Her first novel, *No Clouds of Glory*,
was published in 1968, followed by *The Honeyman
Festival* (1970), *Monodromos* (1973), *Joanne* (1975),
Bear (1976), which won the Governor-General's Award,
The Glassy Sea (1978) and *Lunatic Villas* (1981).
She was the first chairperson of the Writers' Union of
Canada and was appointed an Officer of the Order of
Canada in 1982.

Marian Engel died at the age of 51 in Toronto in 1985.
The Tattooed Woman, a collection of her short stories,
was published posthumously the same year.

MARIAN ENGEL

THE GLASSY SEA

Penguin Books

Penguin Books Canada Ltd., 2801 John Street, Markham, Ontario,
Canada L3R 1B4
Penguin Books Ltd., Harmondsworth, Middlesex, England
Penguin Books, 40 West 23rd Street, New York, New York
10010 U.S.A.
Penguin Books Australia Ltd., Ringwood, Victoria, Australia
Penguin Books (N.Z.) Ltd., 182-190 Wairau Road, Auckland 10,
New Zealand

First published by McClelland and Stewart, 1978

Published in Penguin Books, 1987

Copyright © The Estate of Marian Engel, 1978

All rights reserved.

Manufactured in Canada by Gagne Printing Ltd.

Canadian Cataloguing in Publication Data
Engel, Marian, 1933-
    The glassy sea

Originally published: Toronto: McClelland and Stewart, 1978.
ISBN 0-14-009659-0

I. Title.

PS8559.N44G53 1987   C813'.54   C87-093156-3
PR9199.3.E5G53 1987

For Libby, who lent the
house with the view of
the field; and Pat, Alma,
Hilda, and Reshard, who
made sure I got there.

Although there is, indeed, an Anglican Bishop of Huron, I have never had the pleasure of meeting him or his predecessor. For the purposes of fiction I have simply taken the name of his office in vain. Isaac Hellmuth, however, was a real and most interesting person.

As far as the Eglantine Sisters are concerned, they owe more to a little convent I stayed in in Cyprus, and whose polysyllabic name I never mastered, than to reality. They were Orthodox, and their motherhouse was in Alexandria. "Ancren Riwle" also contributed to the Eglantine foundation; but I have no doubt that if the Eglantines *had* existed, they would have been like this.

In short, no one is intended to resemble anyone alive and breathing; yet coincidences may exist.

Marian Engel

Wer jetzt kein Haus hat, baut sich keines mehr.
Wer jetzt allein ist, wird es lange bleiben,
Wird wachen, lesen, lange Briefe schreiben,
und wird in den Alleen hin und her
unruhig wandern, wenn die Blätter treiben.

—Rilke, "Herbsttag"

THE
GLASSY
SEA

Prologue

They left half an hour ago. Since then I've been sitting in an exhausted reverie. I wonder if I've quite taken in what's happened. But then I have always been fatally slow to react.

Properly, I repeated my arguments. Gallantly, Philip repeated his. I said that my reservations must have consumed much of his time. He said the time had been well spent. The retort courteous.

Even after today's small ceremony, I am not sure that what has been done is right. On the other hand, I am too tired to examine my motives now; and I believe an edge of unsureness engenders honesty. If I hold onto it I shall not be arrogant, which is surely the sin I am most likely to fall into in this position.

Only Philip, the Archdeacon and Anthony were present. I felt strange but comfortable in the old costume. Their voices were clear. They echoed in the chilly silence.

Their clear voices echoing. My mind wanting to stray. I thought, the kneeler is scuffed, if only there were music . . . Mary Rose . . . but I brought myself back.

I refused to have a ring on my finger. Some of them will want them, some of them will want black metal rings like engineers. I won't allow it. We will be what we are, not brides of Christ.

I shall put Philip's beautiful cross in the safe tonight. There shall be no outward and visible sign but plainness.

I feel very strong, very calm, as if grace had indeed been conferred. Perhaps it has. There are miracles. I suppose, though, it's more because now I know who I am and what I want. I see a clear path. I shall pray that it is the right path and that it can be kept clear.

There's that lovely Irish hymn, "Be Thou my Vision. . . ." I should go in and play it on the harmonium.

The reason why music goes with religion, Dr Stern, is that it is also anti-rational.

He used to say to me, "You want things to be black or to be white; you want things to be single and simple. Of course some things are anti- or pre- or post-rational. Of course others are rational. It's a question of putting things in their place." Interesting mind, he had. I didn't expect that in a psychiatrist.

At the end of the ceremony our eyes were all wet with tears. I felt as if I had come home.

I wanted Mary Elzevir to attend, but her doctor was against it. She is ninety and very happy, he said. The glory of God that charges her has split her mind into strange shards, but she is happy.

Mary Rose is dead. I feel . . . idolatrous . . . sitting in her chair. But perhaps Philip is right. One takes strength from office. If one can hold the pride of office at arm's length (without, of course, forgetting responsibility), one can achieve enough goodness to keep one's balance.

After the ceremony, Anthony and Philip and I took a little sherry, the Archdeacon having excused himself. (Which was a relief: he reminded me of Asher.) I lit a fire here in the study.

The house is empty and cold. Philip persuaded me to sit in this big chair. Then he rubbed his hands. "I feel better now."

"Why?"

"Because if I robbed you of a certain amount of your past, I have given you a future."

"How did you rob me of my past?"

"When we first met, remember?"

"At Maggie's? The dinner party when I was pregnant?"

"She put you next to me."

"I remember. She asked me particularly to sit next to someone called Philip Yurn because everyone else was afraid of him."

Anthony roared. "I love Ontario accents."

"Some fear clergymen, others psychiatrists," said Philip.

Anthony blushed. He is always afraid that if he reads Freud, it will remove his vocation. I suspect he will do it himself one day.

"It was so funny," I said. "So like Maggie to get Phoebe up like Primavera to wait at table, then mispronounce your name."

Then we both remembered another moment in our conversation, when he had raised his head high on his long neck and looked down his long nose and said, in his witty bray, "And how does your husband enjoy being married to one who was once the bride of Christ?" and I looked across Maggie's peonies at Asher, and Asher was staring at me, hating me. And Philip saw.

"It wasn't your fault, Philip," I told him. I passed him the little plate of Greek sweetmeats his wife had sent me. Even bedridden, she is capable of such gestures.

"No," he said, "it would be both proud and neurotic of me to consider that what happened was my fault, Mary P. Nevertheless, having witnessed your loss of innocence on that occasion. . . ." He got himself tangled in the nuts in his teeth and failed to continue.

"Tactless," said Anthony.

"Forgiven," I said, raising my glass to him.

11

Anthony looked at us. "I forgot to tell you that the year the brothers decided to have sherry at five every day they were all salivating like dogs by four forty-five."

"A bad habit," I said. And we laughed again.

"So our story will have a happy ending?" Philip asked. He looked old, then, paper-white and tired.

"A happy beginning," I told him.

He kissed me good-bye and left.

Anthony stayed for a while, staring at the fire. Then he said restlessly, "You're not sure, are you?"

"I'm never really sure of anything, Anthony."

"But there's something bothering you, isn't there? Something particular?"

"In a way."

"Don't you think you ought to tell me what it is?"

"I'm not sure I can quite put it into words." I turned so that I, too, could see the fire. That still didn't do. I moved to Philip's chair beside Anthony. "That's better, I'm like a hen on hot coals behind that desk. I don't feel good enough to sit on that chair, that's what's bothering me."

"That you pray about. But something else?"

"Anthony, you're a ferret!"

"Stoat." He said it in a kind of croak. In a way, the word woke me up.

"Women," I said, "that's what it is, women."

"What do you mean?"

"Why should I get my authority from men?"

"There isn't a woman . . . now. There will be."

"Anyway, I think that's what it is."

"It's something. I feel a reservation in you."

"Oh, Anthony, there always will be a reservation in me, if that's what you're worried about. Why do you think she called me Pelagia?"

"Mary Rose? Why?"

"Not for Aphrodite, I can tell you that. Oh, it's my ghastly Puritan background, the perfectionism. I can't work it out of myself. You can't either."

"I'm no Pelagian."

"Don't take umbrage. It was drummed into us both at school and at Sunday school: 'Be ye perfect even as I am perfect.' "

"One can't."

"But one tries. And perfection is death."

"You said it was perfect by the sea."

"It was. But it was a kind of death."

"If you believe in the afterlife, how can perfection be death?" He had turned his full face to me. He looked young and vulnerable. I shall have to watch him, I thought.

"That's a good argument, Anthony," I said in the voice of Mary Rose, "but I think we should take it up another time, don't you?"

He left, then. Now I am alone and amazed. There is a ceremony that confers authority. Authority, like the bird, arrives.

"Do you really believe," my friend Amabel asked, suppressing, respectfully, a snort, "all that stuff?"

I said I didn't know.

I shall never know. That's what is bothering me.

No, what bothers me is that I *do* know. And I am afraid of what I know. I am afraid of being who I am, of being where I am. I was safer, safer by far, down there on the shore. I had nothing to risk and nothing to lose. Now I have power, only a little power, but with power comes risk. I am afraid.

The fire is low now. I'm alone in the creaking house. It feels very queer. Half of me is preoccupied with plans for the future, sorting out the order of the Order, the habit of habits, the rules of the Rule. But the rest of me lingers a little in the past. It's as if I haven't quite walked through the looking glass.

Well, there is much to do, but there is also time. I am in the ridiculous position of being the only Eglantine sister. Oh, I forgot Elzevir, catching mice in the hospital kitchens. Poor ruined soul. The only, then, functioning Eglantine. And before there are more, there is much to be worked out.

Perhaps I will deal with the past before I quite put it away. If our plans come to fruition, it will be useful to know how to put past to yesterday so that remembering is not a pastime pre-occupying the soul forever.

I'll read the letter I wrote to Philip last summer. It will teach me, perhaps, how finally to deal with the disastrous baggage of the past without smugness, without pain.

Oh, are we supposed to be avoiding pain now?

Ladies, I'll hand out no knotted cords.

I'll give myself three hours. Perhaps first I'll make my tea. I'll read in the kitchen while the kettle boils. I hope someone comes who's good at gardening; I'll never get the flower beds in shape myself.

There's no one here but myself to serve me. Funny, self-service in French is *libre-service*. Maybe the other way around. Free service. Service-free?

Unless I misunderstand.

The Letter

Dear Philip Yurn,

I'm sorry I haven't written before, but to tell you the truth I've been busy enjoying myself, and it seemed important to do that when I came here. This is the first day I have even thought to get paper out and take the lid off the typewriter. I have set a card table on the porch so as to be outdoors, which is just as important to me at the moment as enjoying myself. The air is clear, the wind is gentle, the sun on my skin is a blessing: I feel as if I were in one of the hymns about resurrection and quite justified, after all these years, in simply counting my blessings, which have turned out to be many.

This place is perfect for me, I'm sure by accident. Asher must have been looking for a cheap and isolated place, and this is what he found: an old frame farmhouse off an abandoned road leading to a broken dock in a tidal estuary. There are a few houses on the main road north of me, and a couple of summer cottages about half a mile to the west. Otherwise, I am

quite cut off, and would not even have received your letter if
the man who came to see me about business hadn't brought me
a shovel with which to dig a post-hole in the shoulder of the
bank. Then I lugged the mailbox out and stuck it in. Five
minutes later the mailman came by in a red Volkswagen and I
heard from you: hey, presto, complete: one life. As in Life and
Letters, of course.

I am supposed also to use the shovel for clamming. Wonder
if I will? I'm probably too much of an inlander. What bits of a
clam does one eat?

Yes, I think he must have been looking for a cheap, grim,
and isolated place and by a miracle found this. It is shabby and
comfortable, nothing to bother describing, just a farmhouse
like all farmhouses, a summer place like many summer places,
full of old best-sellers, July and August *New Yorkers*, university
textbooks, and Penguin classics. I brought a few books with
me, too, but I haven't been reading much; it's too glaring outdoors, and I have been indulging in a great deal of sloth. I keep
prowling my territory; I have to keep my eyes on it in case it
disappears. I'm like God protecting Bishop Berkeley's tree; if I
don't watch it, the tide won't come in, the estuary won't fill
and empty to its own thrilling rhythm, one that no man but me
can tamper with (I play God, you see!), which is the great advantage of being on salt water: tides perversely choose moon
over clock and liberate their watchers.

Then there are the herons, great grey Japanese shadows
against the sun, grey even if the birdbook calls them blue,
standing eternally on one foot (or another? If I watch them
long enough will I catch one shifting? Is my sight good
enough?) with their sullen eyes and slashing beaks, waiting,
waiting; then: plunge, splash. I am glad they are not my
enemies.

There are ravens, crows, and ordinary field birds; and one
extraordinary bird that rolls himself like the point of a pencil
against the sky all day, soaring higher and higher and making
a strange whistling noise that seems to come not from his beak
but from his wings. I call him sometimes the windhover and

16

sometimes more domestically the goofy bird; for the sound he makes is queer and unromantic.

There are snipe, also, which sit on fenceposts calling back and forth to each other, setting up echoes so that the field rollicks with their sound.

And this field in front of the house is extraordinary as well. I am tempted to say it's a picture, but it is not a picture, that sort of use of English makes me cross; it is a field, but field as I've never seen field before, a wide variegation of greens studded with blue flags, and greens that shift and change in the sea wind, so there are a hundred grass colours; and sometimes my mind's eye interferingly plants it with poppies because it is a Renoir field; but the wind changes again and I see it as it is and it is not full of poppies. The red-orange is hawksbeard, setting off the blue-violet of the iris just as the art teacher at high school said it would. And the ditches are foaming with wild madder (I have been assiduous with the Field Guide), and there are lupins, and the Queen Anne's lace is opening. It is a life's work to keep an eye on the field.

There's a long sort of lump in the middle of the field which my Ontario eye thought was an esker until I realized this island had never been glaciated. The man (Mr Macdonald his name is, like everyone else's here if it isn't Campbell) who does my business or is, to call a spade a spade, my keeper, says it's the last of an old railway embankment, for long ago there was a port in the estuary. But the sides of the quay have fallen in, the port is silted up, and even the lobster sheds have fallen down. And there's a poor little fir tree trying to grow on the railway embankment and not making much of a go of it, though the snipe like it.

As I said, I have been experimenting with sloth. I sleep a lot, and at odd hours. I also go for walks. At low tide I cross the estuary, for the river mouth just covers my ankles, and I am sometimes deliciously startled by crabs scrabbling sideways away from my interloping toes. Then I walk on the rubbery sand and inspect tidal pools, looking for strange things or interesting things or nothing at all: once I saw a dead ray the gulls had been after, and there are little fish like suckers and a lot of crabs and the spoutings of clams. On the sandbar on the far shore there are gulls' nests. I don't go farther than perhaps half a mile, because then there are rocks, and the barnacles and little mussels on these rocks are hell on the feet. Sometimes I just sit and stare at the sea, or lie back in a nest of dry sand at the cliff edge and think of nothing, the way one does when staring into a fire.

There's a complicated series of sandbars in the other direction but there are cottages on the cliffs, and I don't want to see anyone. Human.

When I don't want to go to the beach I go up the road towards the village, which consists, like the one I was born in, of a store, two houses, and a gas station. All the dogs bark at my beggary but I walk on through and a bit farther on there's an old road Macdonald says is called Mac Moan's road, but for no reason he can tell. And Mac Moan's road is full of roses. They came out this week, and all for me. And I stand, surrounded by these roses (once a pick-up truck came careering down and nearly ran over me; it was full of garbage bags so Mac Moan's must also be the dump road but I don't go that far, I am through with going that far) and I think of how we met, and of you.

And so now I write and send you greetings, particularly from these roses.

Last night I went up Mac Moan's in the dusk and stood among the mosquitoes and the roses, trying what we had tried by the river as children, to be Indians and not feel the bites, and I concentrated my whole soul on the roses and thought what were the possible thoughts about roses, starting oddly with Rrrrrose Selavy: Rosasharn, Rosalie, Cicely, Gertrude, Rosamond, Rosa Mundi, only a, and the roses of Picardy and all the roses in all the songs, sick roses, and lo how a rose, Mary Rose of course, our Sister Mary Rose, the Romaunt of the Rose, no, not all the possible: there are limits of the mind, particularly mine, and the fact that one is not, after all, an impervious Indian. I fled. But for one fleeting moment I was back in

18

the rose-world inhaling all the mysteries; I felt the metaphysic and the crowns and the thorns were around me again and I wanted to go into the heart of them all. Dr Stern would be disapproving of this image but there are things he cannot understand. A rose is a woman, perhaps, but also a symbol, a flower, and the symbol of the mystery of the flower, and for me of a place and a life, and though I never became, had the faith or talent or grace to become (and never will have, dear Philip, never will have, you must understand) the Keeper of the Roses, for one moment I was at the heart of the roses and of the universe. And then it evaporated, as orgasms do, which are syntheses also, and I was a bitten woman on a muddy road.

But I understood, I understood. And I remembered, too, all the plashy, plangent things, the halcyon, flashing, glorious images that have attracted me all my life, as some women are drawn to precious stones and others to silks and furs and others to rainbows of children; and the lines of poetry that drew me to the hearts of all the roses; and loving and touching and giving birth. Perhaps, in that moment, I was the rose.

Not Mary; no, Mary is only one incarnation of the rose. One I fear still as a male projection of the floral on the carnal; but perhaps what to some she represented was the stilling of time in the dead centre of the rose garden, and I was there.

Oh, I was seduced early by roses and crowns. You remember, I must have told you. I was a little girl and my name was Rita Heber, R. Heber, and every Sunday in church we started with Hymn Number One, "Holy, Holy, Holy," by R. Heber, and I wrote it, and the golden crowns of the saints were cast in a glassy sea, and tell me how they would that Heber came from Hebert, we were not only country bumpkins, we were French-Canadian country bumpkins, and our line was called the French Line, which is why we could and should amount to nothing, I was in there with the cherubim and the seraphim. I had to be. I knew I belonged there – perhaps only with the splash, perhaps only as audience, but I belonged there.

And now I am by the sea. Have I come home?

Dear Philip, you must realize why I can't do what you ask for the church. I was a child, once, a little female child. I started out with yellow hair and little pink kid shoes with buttons on them, the kind of buttons later used to fix teddy-bears' eyes. I sat in a wicker highchair shoving peas through the seat, the Little One in a white voile dress. My brothers and sister and my parents and the hired man when we had one all fussed over me. Our place was in a bleak field, and at night the garage sign creaked on its hinges in its O, and I grew up to long for better things: a Pegasus or a White Rose, for instance, instead of plain old Imperial, and I wished we had one of those eagles standing on top of the world, or a bear, confusingly, for bearings (a bush for bushings? or Presbyterians?) or at least Blackie with a signboard; but we were plain people, as my mother kept telling me. Macraes and Hebers had been on this line for 150 years, there was no nonsense, no romance about people with such staying power. Even if, in the little back field my father never managed to make himself sell, not even for my education or Shirl's wedding, there hung, on a little wrought-iron frame from a rusty chain, a stone heart engraved faintly with the words "Our Baby," which the rust had dropped tears on: I come of a plain people not made for mysteries.

In that part of the world, the Indians were for mysteries. They had mysterious church services they invited the United Church girls to (The Canadian Girls in Training, but I have forgotten what, in a white middy, for) and invoked spirits at; and bred enormously and illegitimately and hid guns in kettles and disappeared into the swamps. Their children went not to our schools but to mission schools. They knew things, we didn't know things. You ask any of us, there aren't many of us left: on the French Line we didn't hold with mysteries. I can't take care of roses, Philip.

It was Aunt Mary Hunter, across the road, whose husband Uncle Doog (never Doug, I don't know why) ran the store, who grew the roses, though she wouldn't lift a finger to count out humbugs to a crippled child. And she was famous in the county for her stocks and foxgloves. She was tall and fair. She used to like to brush my hair in the sunlight, so it would be fair like hers; just let me put some sunshine in it, she would say. While my mother was baking and patching and mending, trying to make ends meet on the money a poor man brought in who fixed cars and combines and tractors and had been gassed in what they all called the last war. Auntie Mary, she had no children. Nooooo children. No one to annoy her. She could afford to grow roses. On what Doog charged for that lumpy bakery bread.

She had a long face and a fur coat and a diamond ring, Auntie Mary. I wasn't supposed to love her, but I did; children choose their own families; you must never tell them who's bad and who's good. I was scared of my Grammacrae, the epitome of one who's long in the tooth. She looked like the wolf in the bed on Little Red Riding Hood and believed in Divide and Rule. From her bed up at Uncle Bill's and Aunt Jean's she kept a firm hold on her family by pitting them against each other. She was my great-grandmother, actually, but Mother's mother had died when she was born, or when Millie was born, I forget which, and Grammacrae had raised, it seemed, half the township. I was supposed to love her, but she had one milk-white eye. She didn't look very safe to me and whenever I saw her I hid under something. I loved Auntie Mary instead.

I was, you see, perverse. Left-handed, too. I drove my mother wild. She said Mary bribed me with humbugs (it was little pink fondant doves) and fed me when she shouldn't, and I mustn't go over to that Mary's who thought she was so good, any more; until my father started coughing again, which was what always stopped Mother's flights of fancy.

Plain folks, country people, Hebers and Macraes. The original Hebers had been Catholics but by now they'd mostly seen the light and come over to our side, fortunately, else my parents would never have been allowed to marry, or I'd have grown up with my hair parted in the middle like Tessie McCrory around the corner up the concession line, black Irish Catholic, though Jack was a good farmer, you could say that about him, but I wish he'd get his bugger of a fly-wheel fixed in town properly. And the priest would have let the mother die while the baby lived, which is why we were all lucky it happened long ago, that Hebers started marrying Macraes and not McCrorys, so that on both sides of the family there were red Hebers and black Hebers, red Macraes and black Macraes, though for some reason that bothered me I'd come out on the beige side. Walters were red Hebers, which is maybe why he beat Millie with a blackthorn stick, and she lit out down the road with the three youngest one day and that was the end of that, never marry a man because he's a good dancer.

Good country people. Mud in the spring up to our ankles and walking along the frozen rutted road to school in winter, it was washboardy in both directions, criss-crossed corduroy, you could break your head on it if you fell and you took your knees out of your stockings again, dirty girl, and there's Mickey's house, where he died, all fallen in, ghosts in the lilacs runnnn-nnn.

All the ghosts had the names of the unsaved Irish.

Heavy clay land, that. Stuff forcing itself up through the soil had a time of it. Father was meant to farm but he liked machines better, would have made a go of it after tractors came, but following a horse's ass up and down a furrow . . . (now Frank!) so he sold the west half of the farm to Peacock and kept the corner part, house, barn, garage; and the field where Stu kept the old blind horse he won at cards that got struck by lightning and I dreamed about it, night after night, a white horse and a thunderbolt coming down and the blinkered thing not knowing: oh, it bothered me.

We had cats in the barn but only in the house if the mice were bad, except Pinky, the albino, who lived in, but had a great unwillingness to play.

Doog had Holsteins and Aunt Mary for all her finery used to sit in the woodshed and work the barrel churn. They all wore funny business-like shoes, then, for their backs, and for boredom she put her hands to her waist, and she looked as odd as the word akimbo. And I thought buttermilk would be so good, the way my father came around for it like a hummingbird after hollyhocks, but it wasn't. "Ah," he'd exhale. "Mary, buttermilk!" And it tasted awful.

We had electric light but they didn't over on the Home Farm, Grammacrae's and Bill's and Jean's; there was an old grouch that was a holdout on the line and it was well on into the war (the second, not the last) that they got it over there and stopped rubbing up lamp chimneys and pumping water by hand. They were relieved: it meant you could leave children under twenty alone in the house, and not take them all to all the meetings.

We had our own old grouch up the end of our line, where the road stopped at Birch Creek (not a birch to be seen, all scrub hawthorn and willow), Uncle Eddie, who ran the little cable ferry for the government, that was cheaper than building a bridge. You sat in your Ford or your Chev or your Rockney and honked, and Eddie wound the cable slowly over, and you drove onto the barge, which some kind of machine then hauled over to the other side. I hated Eddie. His wife had left him and I knew why. My mother sent me to him with baskets of cakes and pies. He could have got food from Doog or the neighbours but none of them was speaking to him. I'd have to go over with my basket, Little Eva on the ice, and he looked all right, pink and clean, but I knew that first he'd look in to see if I'd got over the creek without breaking anything (there were stepping stones and fallen trees and islands, a child doesn't need the ferry) and then he'd put his arm around me and tell me what a good girl I was and try to get his finger up my pants. I hated him, but I knew if I told my mother she'd think I'd invited it or invented it, and anyway my father wasn't big enough to beat him up, not with gassy lungs; and when I saw in the paper he'd died, I was spitefully glad. He lived to be eighty-seven because he hectored the government for a free heart-pacer. If I were the government I'd never have given him one. I'm still unrepentant about Eddie.

I've just remembered another thing about roses, a poem we had in school. I fancy it was Browning but it probably wasn't. It began, "It was roses, roses all the way. . . ." It was about a hero, and something bad happened, too. We had a lot of poetry in school and a lot of British history, with a little Brébeuf and Lalement here and there on the side.

Why, I wonder, did the rose become the valuer, the circle's pure symbol? Because it didn't last? Was perfumed? Blowzy? Life-cycle like a woman's body, tight, then ripe, then in the end, drooping and loose? Rare? No, it was everywhere. Age-old, though. Scented. Flavoured. The sickliness of Turkish Delight. And, in the north, temporary. And, ah yes, enthorn-ed, thus enthroned.

"Why," Dr Stern wanted to know, "did you become a nun?" He had more than a psychiatric interest. I suppose his mind, too, was impregnated with the mysteries of nuns' tales, the in-evitable sexuality that clings to the asexual.

"It wasn't hard," I said, "to think of living a life of poverty, chastity, and obedience where I came from."

That wasn't the reason, though. I wanted roses and was will-ing to endure what I thought would be the thorns. I wanted to escape the world, though the Order was, in terms of what I grew up in, extremely worldly.

We were plain country people, Methodists until 1925 and Church Union. (There were continuing Presbyterians around still, and Free Methodists too, with their predestination and tongues of fire, but good anti-Catholic Grit was good enough for us.) We were not poor, for, as it was pointed out, there was good plain food on the table. Our clothes were not new, but they were in order, and it gave one a feeling of generation to be buttoned by Mother's cold bony fingers into a cotton waist which had held up the winter stockings of a dozen other lit-tle Macraes and Hebers male and female, for none of us was forced to hold up our stockings with elastic, which was lower class, though the boys soon graduated to breeks. I wore waists in the winter and brown stockings and big navy blue cotton overpants made of sweatshirt material that felt like silk on little red legs, and navy blue tunics and white blouses that had seen other children, too, but never had holes in them, and I had a red cardigan with tulips on its black buttons that I had licked

24

all the coloured paint off. And innumerable Red River coats with tassled belts I lost, and red mittens with long, long thumbs that I sucked snow out of until I wet my warm wool snowpants: We were not poor.

We had food, we had clothing, we had heat. My father's shovel grated early on the cellar floor, and the dust made him cough, and Mother shook Kenny and Stu to go down and help him, and the day began.

But I live in unutterable luxury here, for the wind is like silk and I can think of roses. And the strange bird winds his way up in the sky, and I can think of him any way I want: he is anything, everything, a bird (himself), or a symbol. I have chosen to let him be himself. I have set him free. He means nothing but his own song.

You know: I think back there one was a child. One lived in a piggy infant world. I used to lick and sniff my way through it every day, sitting in Peacock's grain store (why was I there?) in a bin of buckwheat, running the strange three-sided grains over my summer legs; or letting the calves lick my salty knees half raw in Doog's old barn; or lying somewhere in the crook of a snakefence corner, they were calling me, I was bad, I would not go, I had found caterpillars and I had let them run all over me; had to pick them off one by one before I went in for supper, then lie about how I got the itch.

And in school I ran my nose up and down the foolscap trying to feel the lines until they sent for the eye doctor; and I ate paste and smelled the glue of the new readers and nipped corners of thick-paged English books, and shifted a bolo ball from cheek to cheek till the teacher cried, "Dirty girl," and shook me till I cried myself.

I was the baby, the youngest. Shirley was six when I was born, a grand help in the kitchen, and the boys were older, just old enough for the war Kenny never came home from and they didn't even give Mother a star for the window like the ones in the *Saturday Evening Post* (Auntie Mary took it, we had *Maclean's* and *Saturday Night*, we were patriots). And my father was the oldest child of all, carefully watched over, sssshhhh don't disturb him, and the ghost of the gassed horseman came up out of the trenches underneath the floor and shone his teeth at us.

Underworld is innate. Every child knows it and fears the cellar stairs. Down cellar behind the axe is the cistern, mossy, forbidden; the fruit cellar is dry, but behind the new fruit is the old, which has been there forever, and there are bad apples in every barrel ("Spies for pies!" she'd sing out, sending me down), and there was a corner by the cistern where something mouldy and rubbery hung and that was where I knew the mome raths outgrabe.

The wind came from the west, from across the American border (fools to blame their weather on us) where the big houses were on the other bank of the big river, another country, Michigan, that my second cousin once removed, Mel, ran the international ferry to, that his mother was always boasting about in sentences beginning "My Mel." The winter wind came with Mel's ferry and once when I was very small they put me down on the step and turned to lock the door, and the wind picked me up like a kite and blew me along the frozen crust of the snow. They had, they said, the devil's own time getting me back, but I don't remember. It's only a tale from the time of buttoned shoes.

It was the wind under the earth that blew when we had the earthquake that I slept through. That bothered me. It must come out of the holes, I thought, out of the fruitcellars and rootcellars, no matter where Dorothy hid; and it was real, because the day after the earthquake a little brown and white dog turned up at Mary and Doog's (not our house, alas, or was it turned away?), right, as they said, out of the blue. And I knew, I knew.

I knew because in summer you could walk along the road and listen to the underground streams that the Nazis sent their messages through in little folded paper boats: you could hear them, sometimes they made a sound like Morse code. If you lay flat on the dirt road (dirty girl, dirty girl!) you could hear those creaking, buzzing, trickling underground sinister streams as sure as you could hear the furnace beating like a heart under the school when you put your head on the desk.

I was the youngest. There were the three others, Shirley always by my mother's side until she took up lipstick and going out with soldiers and sailors – then the fat was in the fire – and Kenny away and dead almost before I knew him, but something went out of them; and Stu, my black-hearted brother Stu, the one who's the printer in, of all the bombed-out places, Detroit, though he wasn't always like that, just mostly.

"Ash Bone," he said when I told him I was married. "Ash Bone. That dirty bastard son of a Tory bagman, lace on his pants. Kid, you'll get what you asked for." I hope he isn't right about everything.

Oh, we gave them a time, we did. My father was permanently tired from that war, and my mother had fallen arches from being permanently compared unfavourably by Grammacrae to her sisters, not one of which she was inferior to in any way. What they wanted was a bit of peace so they could listen to the war news and Citizens' Forum, but we nagged and pestered them. They were unlike: he was small, she was big; he was dark, she was fair; he was cool, she had a temper that picked her up and danced with her. We caught their differences and gave them little to smile at. He'd been no heck in school, he said, but he could fix anything from a separator to a bomber (and he did, when he got that good job in the war) and she'd been to secretarial school in Toronto, but had a breakdown and had to leave, which is how she met him, not in West China Township at all, but in Toronto where his mother was living, who remarried after his father and two brothers died all in one year, 1916, though it hadn't spoiled her. She was a soft-skinned blue-eyed lady who smelled nice and wasn't fearsome. She'd been a good farmer's wife but hadn't cared for the life, so when her chance came she married a Toronto man. My father came home from the war not to the farm but to her house on

Concord Avenue, and one night he went to church with her and ran into Mother, who was recovering with her cousin Hilda who was at Varsity, and boarded around the corner.

My grandmother Heber was soft and pretty. Widowers had a habit of marrying her, so she went through a number of names. People were always dying on her but it didn't make her bitter. She got prettier. The only things that bothered her were the stepdaughters coming to claim things after the funerals, even her own mother's engagement ring.

Mother and Father decided to go back to the country. I don't quite know why. His health, maybe. The land, the house. The fact that he could make a living there, tinkering with things. Mother always said we were good plain country people, Toronto was no place for us. There was some mysterious curse city life laid on the expatriates of West China Township. Not everyone had Grandma Heber's nice nature and could escape it. So I was born on the West China shore.

Plain, simple people, we were: that was our pride. The church was plain. It had brown pews and you stuck to the varnish in summer; and it had walls the colour of pee (it was hard to choose a colour; nobody used white then because it showed the dirt, and blue was Catholic and pink was hardly Christian. So there were only yellowy-beige and green left, and wasn't green Anglican?) and fogged yellow and white glass windows except for the one at the end which was to the Macrae ancestors of course, the Light of the World in a nightgown but with a splendid border of blue and red; and on one side, a pallid knight, drooping in dusty armour, holding, of course, a rose; to an uncle of ours who had died in that first or last war, the one where they got over all the poems about the Light Brigade.

We sang, though, in that church. Oh, we sang. It was the hymns that made the theology, not the preaching, which was so often done by temporary ministers, or students with many charges, men in black gowns with tabs for ties, so that they looked like professors, but not quite. It wasn't they who made the church, even when we had a whole half-share in one of our own with East China, it was the hymns. We flung them out like the banner, and my cousin Zoe pounded the pump organ to keep up a good pace and fight a good fight against silence and inanition while Isaac Watts and C. and J. Wesley and R. Heber and the Rev. Sabine Baring-Gould (oh, if we had known he collected limericks!) and the Scotch Psalter taught us all we'd ever need to know: when we sang, we sang as one foundation.

I liked it in church after I got over being bored and little and ashamed of the colour of the walls. I felt good there. My mother had fur cuffs on her Sunday coat, and when I was bored or tired or plain hungry for the feel of them, I put my face on her arm and felt and felt. Shirl sang in the choir (Kenny did too, they say, but I don't remember) though never a solo, and her black gown hung off her breasts just so, and her mouth was a scarlet O for the anthem. And my father was an elder and served the communion, passing around the little clattering cups of grape juice and the cubes of bread on silver trays, and though I knew he was thinking how to do it more efficiently, because he told me once, when we sang, "Here, O my Lord, I see Thee face to face," I did, I think, once or twice, or thought I did. I was translated without transubstantiation.

I liked it in church, too, because (you must forgive this, Philip, it is heresy; Asher and I often argued about it and he was continually shocked) I thought I understood Jesus. I didn't understand any of the other people I had read about because they did unheard-of things like get caught in lobster pots or vanish down rabbit holes, or were orphans, but there was He, born in a barn, child of a man who worked with his hands (and my father, too, would have walked miles in winter to be honest and pay his taxes) and a woman who obviously worked her fingers to the bone. And, like me, He asked a lot of questions. I was always asking questions.

I knew I was a girl, but that hardly seemed relevant. Girls did girls' things, but my Mum put on Dad's mackinaw when he was sick and a horn blew outside and, unlike Auntie Mary, pitched in, trudged out and pulled the lever on the gas pumps so the blue-green gas went gurgle into the tanks of the cars; and so, later, did I, and I could wipe a fine windshield, too, shovel a walk, muck out a pigpen up at Uncle John's when all the boys were away at the war, and I also went to school: sure, I could ask questions. I didn't get anywhere with them, but aside from the fact that He was the Messiah and I wasn't, I didn't see that there was much difference between me and Jesus.

Oh dear, I'm afraid I've never lost the feeling. Imagine the arrogance of countenancing the feeling that one is as good as God. And I failed so early to distinguish God's masculinity from my feminity, ill-defined as it was by red cardigans and Kitty Higgins bows, that I became, in spite of my instincts, which are on the whole as passive as any man could wish, a woman of my own generation. And this failure, of course, has caused infinite sorrow to all of us, for the boys, raised to believe they were certainly superior, have had to deal with women they were unable to prove their superiority to except by one exhausting act. And the women, secure in their feeling of equality when they left home, were insecure in their femininity: lie back to embrace frailty as they would, they could not unless they were drunk or diseased.

For the women I grew up with were not frail: they had their bunions, their miscarriages, their preferences – like Aunt Mary not waiting on customers in the store – but Mother and my aunts routinely worked, as they said, their fingers to the bone, and thought, because they belonged to a puritanical religion and an even more puritanical culture, that it was right to do so. They were glad to work and scorned luxury. They knew that during the courting period girls had to pay lip-service to the kind of titivation fashion magazines encouraged, and they knew this because they actively pitied their unmarried cousins who did not have homes of their own. Old snapshots often show them as rather muscular brides – though Grammacrae had a horror of freckled girls and made everyone wear sun bonnets – but, as the qualities the boys were taught to look for in a woman were those shared by ploughhorses (solidity, calm, lack of temperament), the externalized femininity of the fashionable world was as far from our world as the farther reaches of the real China were from West China Township.

I certainly, at the age of twelve or thirteen, disapproved of the world of fashion magazines, which Shirl sneaked into the house. I saw that if I followed the logic of my training I would have to deal with it, but the idea of coating my fingernails with a foreign substance made me shudder. I couldn't see why, if God put hair on my legs, He also required me to lop it off. Similarly, if He had given me straight hair – but He didn't, and it was my one victory, I was the one girl in West China who never had a Toni Home Permanent – I'd have objected to curling it. My pre-adolescent judging eye passed over my sister Shirley with her bobby pins and papers soaked in ammonia, her lipstick, her hidden supply of mascara, and rejected the image. She may have wanted to look like a movie star, but I knew that real class was all wool and a yard wide.

That Shirley's often smuggled equipment (for Mother had mysterious taboos: lipstick, yes, mascara, no) was an outward and visible sign of an inward and seething sexuality never occurred to me. I could not, and still really do not, understand flouncy night-dresses that leave your shoulders cold, though now, of course, I know more than I should about why they are worn. Lace, Mother explained as she carefully picked it off slips and pyjamas Grandma Heber gave us for Christmas, all wrapped in Eaton's fancy paper with real ribbon and imitation poinsettas on the bows, was something that got torn in the wringer. Fancy goods Didn't Last, and that was that. If you took Jesus seriously, you wanted things that moth and rust would not corrupt: I quite approved of that principle. Shirl didn't.

It was on that principle, too, that I disapproved of, and was intolerably confused by, and I was not the only one in the family to be confused by, the wife Stu brought home in the fall of '43. He had been stationed in Quebec and he brought home this girl – and his son. My God. Bells rang, signals flashed. Stu, constant all his life in his desire to crush any kind of parental approval, had done it again. Her name was Mariette and

31

she was not what Mother and Grammacrae would call refined; she had big hips and a huge bosom, and between them a tiny waist. She wore a maroon gabardine suit and maroon lips and nails to match, and her hair was a complication of sausage rolls with a doily on top. She wore high, high heels and I think perhaps even platform soles and an ankle strap, but I certainly remember her stockings, for they had a seam up the back as sooty as eyebrow pencil, and so straight she must have spent half an hour putting them on. Stu carried the baby, looked my parents straight in the eye (having given them no notice, simply arrived on a Sunday night, knowing they would be home) and said, "Hi, folks, this is my wife, Mariette." Holy jumped-up Judas, which was my father's only public oath.

Stu had done it this time. A flagrant female and a French-Canadian at that. Catholic, no doubt about it. I mean, she even looked Catholic: dark hair and bold eyes.

First she hesitated, uncertain, a little scared. Then she looked around the kitchen and I knew she didn't like what she saw. It's a shock to marry a foreigner and discover you've married something no better than what you came from yourself. She told us she was from a farm near Shawinigan, and I've often thought that since she was one of nine, not counting the two that had died, our place must have looked empty and austere. The pattern was off the kitchen linoleum, a sign to us that my mother kept a clean floor; to her it must have been poverty.

And when that no-better-than-what-you've-come-from-yourself turns cold as ice at the sight of you. . . .

Mother, in fact, turned scarlet, but she did not violate the rules of hospitality. She put the kettle on right away and then leaned over the baby to coo over him. Drew back from the smell of ammonia. Mariette laughed. "Jesus, the little bugger shits all the time," she said. "Go get a diaper, Stu."

I was sent to bed and I went with great reluctance since Mariette kept saying, "Oh, let the kid stay up, I like her," hoping, I suppose, that I'd be on her side. Shirl was still out. I lay for a long time on the floor, listening through the register, shivering, thinking, I wish they'd let me pick the baby up, though I didn't like the way it smelled either ("Such a long ride in the car, poor thing," I heard my mother say. "Bless his little heart.") and waiting for the ruckus to begin.

Stu and Dad exchanged small talk about engines and what was going on at Stu's base. He was ground crew somewhere in Quebec where the zombies were. He hadn't been able to get overseas to die with Kenny. There was something wrong with his eyes and we only sent the fittest. Mother and Mariette somehow got the baby cleaned up and overhauled and Mother put food out and said he was lovely, fancy, she was a grandmother, but I didn't hear any conviction and neither, I bet, did Mariette. Then she asked right out if Mariette was a Catholic and Mariette said sure, and Mother said, "Are you going to turn?" and Mariette said, "Christ, no!" and then there was only the sound of eggs and bacon frying.

"Now Ellner," my father said in the voice he used for her, as if he were trying to sooth a balky horse.

Spoons in cups. The baby sucking and glugging. Finally, dishes being put in the sink, and Mother and Mariette coming upstairs trying to arrange somewhere for the baby to sleep. Mariette yawning and Mother, unexpectedly tender, saying she'd get her the hot water bottle. Mariette giggling: "Stu's enough for me."

Mother went downstairs and told Stu to take the suitcases up, the poor girl was exhausted. She hoped the baby wouldn't mind sleeping in a drawer but no doubt it had seen worse. "Lay off, Mum," Stu growled.

Shirl, always the nicest of us (where does good nature come from, Philip?), bounced in from her date and went into a kind of cheerleader's tango at the idea of having a sister-in-law and a nephew. When she was informed they were French-Canadian she said, "They're really nice people, we're reading *Maria Chapdelaine* in school, can we call the baby Ti-Jacques?" Nothing would stop her bounding upstairs to embrace them. I envied her her enthusiasm.

Then, after Mariette was supposed to be asleep, the Hebers sat down and had a serious talk. "I'm sure she seems very nice,

Stu, but you'll have to be careful, or before you know it you'll have seven children, and you with no trade."

"Mariette don't want seven children."

The slip in grammar appalled her. We spoke right in our house. "What will you do after the war if you can't even speak proper English?"

"Don't you worry. I'll be all right. How do you like her? Ain't she a peach?"

Poor Stu ought to have known better than to bring peaches home out of season.

There was much hemming and hawing and evading of Stu. I thought I'd freeze by the register. Shirl was snoring in her bed. "Well," Father said, "she's a Catholic."

"I'm surprised at you for going out with a Catholic girl," Mother said.

"News for you, Ma," Stu said. "There aren't any Protestants where she comes from."

"Then you might have controlled yourself. Or at least let us know before. Stuart, you'll be the death of me."

I heard him scrape back his chair. I heard my father say, "Now Ellner." I heard Stu growl back, "It's all right, Dad, she can't help being what she is."

Mother gasped.

"You don't like the look of her, do you?" Stu said. "You think she just trapped poor old innocent me. You think she's an idol-worshipper and a gold-digger, eh? You want her to go around looking like death on earth like everyone around here, eh? Well, don't worry about her upsetting your apple cart, Ma. You won't see no more of us."

And we didn't. When I got up for school Monday morning they were gone. "Without a word of thanks or an address," Mother complained half-heartedly. But I knew she was hurt and worried and half-relieved that now Mary and Doog and Jean and Bill and Auntie Hilda and Eddie and Walter would remain a while in ignorance of this disgrace.

Oh, Philip, she couldn't help having the standards of her time and place; and she knew something, too, which was that a big bomb of a woman like Mariette wouldn't spend all her life with a little fellow like Stu, and she was right. Six months later, when he was transferred to Edmonton and wasn't allowed to take her, she ran away with a salesman to the States, taking the baby with her. And he never gave up hunting for her, spent all his care and money trying to find her and his child, but did not succeed. So some of my mother's bigotry was compassion, wasn't it?

Oh, the tumult and confusion of those years between child and adult, the judging and avoiding. I will be. I will never be. Not knowing how little will had to do with it. Our lives were church and school and family. We never stayed in hotels; there were cousins all over Canada, some even in Michigan and Florida. We even had an aunt called Orpha in Newfoundland who sounded like the lady who sliced out the codfish tongues. We stayed within our own frame: our social life was the family and the church, and in our limited way we were very happy.

The cousins I liked best lived further up the river in a pretty village now dismantled in favour of a chemical plant. There were two boys, Bob and Ron, I was a little soft on, and my cheerful aunt and my handsome uncle: I think he was the oldest of Mother's brothers, the favourite. He was also sheriff of the county, which made him both prosperous and romantic. The daughter, Betty, was more Shirl's age, about five years older than me. I loved it at their house because they wanted a child to spoil. They had a pony, they had bicycles, they had all the Burgess Bedtime Story books, and I was happy there.

The only trouble was, on Sundays they went to the Church of England, and I went with them. And when it came time to kneel, the ghost of Oliver Cromwell tapped me on the shoulder and hissed, "Never." Betty saw me hesitate. "Never mind, Rita, I'm not kneeling either. I don't want to get holes in my new nylons." I plunked on the bench as hard as I could. I had understood heresy but I had not yet understood charity.

Do you understand now why I'm impossible, Philip?

I liked that little church, though. So, later, did old Mr Laidlaw, and the summer he tutored me we often went there.

35

Father pointed out to me that the Anglicans, respectable Protestants though they were, had never been "workers," and, true to the history in our textbooks, had clung to their English origins longer than was seemly for Canadians. They had been in favour of the establishment of their church as the official one in Canada, but strangely unalert to the needs of the real people, farmers, fishermen and workers. Whatever else you could say about the Catholic priests now, they had gone out among their people, and the Methodist circuit riders, those heroes of our history books, who, if my mother was to be believed, had led the Rebellion of 1837, had done so too. Rebellion was not to be approved except in cases where the State was trying to ram Anglicans down your throat or keep elected members out of Parliament.

So it was made clear that the Church of England was, however attractively dressed in white or green, however prinked out with chalices and plate from England, politically suspect. Who could, after all, even entranced by the inexplicable grace of altarcloths over plain wood and nautical wall plaques over yellow plaster, approve of the retrograde colonialism of an institution that had supported the Clergy Reserves? Once my knees learned to bend, my ears sang with the poetry of the service. I was then, as I am now, fatally seducible by ear and eye.

Sister Mary Rose used to point out frequently the way in which my love of beauty distracted me from spiritual things, and of course she was right. This is why, I suppose, artists tend to heresy: they live too much for the sensuality of vision. And yet, if the world exists in aesthetic forms, as it clearly does where I am now – for even without the white spire in the distance and the row of firs that shield the farm on the horizon, the place would still be beautiful – what's wrong with letting it please our eyes? I can accept a good many kinds of asceticism, Philip, but I've never seen why it was Christian to choose the ugly over the beautiful if they were both the same price. I'm willing to bet that from most anchorites' caves there was a view.

In fact I grow more and more suspicious of spiritual valuations, Philip. Time wins me away from the diamond of the soul. How can we know another's soul except by his actions, and when his actions cannot be judged except by inexperienced standards, is judgement by appearances altogether false? Or do I drag myself away from what I am really talking about?

I do not believe that beauty is truth, truth beauty. Asher was the most beautiful man I had ever seen, and, you know, I knew him long before I had met him at Maggie Hibbert's; he went to the same high school I did. I saw him first coming out of Mr Martin's trig class as I was coming out of the girls' locker room. I was in grade nine. He was a vision of the perfect knight: tall, fair, grey-eyed, severe in profile. He wore perfect grey trousers, an open-collared white shirt and a navy blue cashmere sweater. Looked neither to left nor right, went down the stairs. I knew he had just come to our school from some boarding school, and that he was the judge's son, Judge Bowen's boy, home because his mother was dying. The sight of him pierced me. I knew then what men should be. I was wrong, but so was my brother Stu when he made his political judgement of him.

In these relationships, with the church up the river that was prettier than ours, with Ash, who was prettier than any man I had ever seen, I made a visual judgement, and also a snobbish one. It is the latter I find hard to forgive. I suppose this kind of snobbery is a desperate longing for self-improvement, but years later when Tessie McCrory told me I was a snob, all of us Macraes were snobs, I knew what she meant. We were indoctrinated in our youth with the fact that we were Good People, and that Good People were United Church, hard-working, teetotal, plain, honest, and sexually virtuous. I have since met people whose slate of family values included a set of silverware and regular visits to the orthodontist. My keeper informs me that social standing here is based on one's acreage in potatoes. My snobbery was to draw away from these values and add a kind of aesthetic romance to them. I suppose growing up is simply a process of successfully incorporating one's inculcated values with those one finds oneself among, and I never have managed it. Too many cymbals clash.

Everything was simple when the singing of the electric wires denoted spies sending underground messages on paper boats, but by the time I got Shirl's high school books to re-cover in brown Bank of Montreal paper wrappers, and got on the bus to go to high school in town, everything had become intolerably complicated. For if Tessie thought we were snobs, at high school I learned we were country bumpkins.

If Shirley hadn't worked in the school office, I don't think I'd have survived. It was the time of see-through nylon blouses and big breasts, and she had those, and also an engagement ring from Ernie. She was boarding with Auntie Hilda in town. By the time I got to school I'd be dizzy from the loud freezing or boiling hour on the bus and the smell of rubber boots, and Shirl would meet me with a cup of hot coffee in the hall or the locker room. She showed me around and told me how to keep in good with which teachers, which wasn't a problem since I was fiercely good academically (I had nothing to do but homework). None of the Heberville children I had known well were in my form. Several had chosen not to go to high school at all and had simply stayed behind to serve time in grade eight until they were sixteen. A couple of others boarded with relatives in town, transforming themselves from country into town mice at once. Others who lived over the town line had gone to high school in another district. And one poor boy called Wilmer had drowned himself so he wouldn't have to leave home.

I often wished I had done it. The twenty-mile ride with the wild ones pelting each other and the bus driver with sandwiches lasted for five years. I crouched in the back with my Latin, hoping against hope there was an eventual moral equivalent of the ablative absolute.

I read recently that the high school years are the ones that create one's mature socialization. I suppose if I'd been Shirley this would have happened. But I was limited by my distance from the school, never able to stay after for tea dances and games, and although even while gas was rationed our verandah was festooned with boys looking for Shirl, no similar fate awaited me. I don't think I really expected it, for you couldn't have dragged me into a see-through blouse if you tried. I wasn't, like Shirl, able to brush away the messages from the underground streams and from Grammacrae and Mother that said boys lead you down and not up. And I didn't know where I wanted to go except that it was up. It was as vague as that, but as strong.

Shirl came home on weekends and gave Mother all the town gossip and me a lot of advice I didn't take about makeup. I had no money for makeup and wouldn't have asked for it. She and Mum got along well then, for she was engaged to her soldier, and though there were rows about the time he brought her home, they also sat for hours and talked about what men call women's things, and I would look up astounded from Latin or history, spellbound by the fact that my mother had gone out with other people than my father, or that she had had a pink chiffon dress once; that she'd lost a baby between Shirley and Stu and cried and cried, for it was a girl, white and waxy. It had opened its little eyes and sighed and died. It had a weak heart. She'd never cried so much in her life except when Kenny died and when Stu brought That Mariette home.

Gradually, the big world of high school (actually, we called it "collegiate" but the word seems to have died now) took over from the small world of home. Slowly, I lost my fear of undressing in the steamy locker room for gym, among the big girls who had thighs like Percherons and busts they made stick way, way out with a kind of brassiere my mother said caused cancer, that had a wide band below it and laces they pulled tight, tight and tighter, as if they were Scarlett O'Hara. Compared to them I was a minnow, and looked at least less ridiculous in the terrible blue bloomer suits we wore, which were inspected with military precision for cleanliness every week. As Mother didn't wash on the weekend, mine were suspect until it occurred to me I could do them by hand myself. I always liked being looked after.

Gym was the only thing I got a D in. I was a puddler, getting dressed and undressed, and the teacher had a mean tongue. She called me Sardine, and the Late Rita. Finally, after she asked me if I combed my hair with an egg beater and I cried, Shirl forged a note for me saying I couldn't take gym because my heart was bad, so that was that.

Shirl used to take me to Woolworths for lunch sometimes, too. She took big-sistering seriously. I began to turn her down when I discovered the public library and a librarian who saw I had a mind and wanted to form it, and turned me off soapy romances and onto Virginia Woolf.

Oh, this is nonsense; it can't interest you. There were a thousand others in that high school who were more interesting. (But only one, perhaps, who became an Eglantine sister by mistake. And I have to tell you this so you'll understand how, later, I married that perfect profile my brother Stu called Ash Bone, and how, eventually, I wrote "non-conformist" on the hospital form when I went to have Chummy. Which is why I cannot do what you ask.)

So, I went to high school, I went from listening to the underground streams to reading through the library; I stood up with Shirl when she married her Ernie and cried when she handed me her bouquet so she could put on her ring, me in orchid voile next to her two best friends in peach and lime. I lived through her first pregnancy as if it were mine and then went back to Virginia Woolf when the baby didn't look very interesting. I also read a book about Freud and dreams and wondered why ships and shoes were sealing wax. And, last child at home, I watched my parents grow close, so close their voices became interchangeable.

What else did I do? I can't really say I remember. I am astonished at how dim that period of my life is now. There is a certain glaucous coating on the emotional memory, the ineradicable smell of rubber boots, but the years from thirteen to nineteen no longer distinguish themselves one from another. Everything is vague.

Who was I? What did I want? I had no idea. I had somehow, I think, expected that, as for Shirley, the verandah would for me also be festooned with boys from the time I was fourteen; but when that did not happen, I cannot say I roared with grief. "You don't have a come-hither eye," Mother said, and I accepted her judgement contentedly.

What I remember most about those years, however, was their isolation. People whose books and articles I read now, praising country life and its ecological sanity, have forgotten or never known how lonely it was to be a country child. Up at dawn to ride the bus to the distant high school. Lunch with the other commuters in a sordid classroom (permeated for five whole years with the smell of Billy Parkin's sardine sandwiches), unable to take part in sports, the school show, the school magazine, even dances: the buses were always leaving. Home to homework and chores. If you wanted to phone anyone the call was long distance and forbidden; if you wanted to see anyone, you had miles to walk in the dark on a rutted and spooky road.

The years slipped painlessly by, but they were not sociable.

There were a few diversions. I went to Young Peoples' at the church for a couple of years. One of the boys got a crush on me, and, walking me home, rubbed his body against me in a field. I quit to avoid him. Once, too, Jean and Billy's Reid took me to a dance at a pavilion on the Lakeshore. It was a soft summer night, and I loved the music and the wind when we went outside. But we were shy of each other.

I suppose it would have been better for me if I'd been friends with Tessie McCrory, who lived not half a mile away and was exactly my age. Alas, Tess was a Catholic and boarded all week at the convent of the Sacred Heart. Sometimes I saw her in the village on weekends and said a rather sulky hello. When we were little we played jacks on the step of Doog's store, but we didn't go to each other's houses. The McCrorys were Catholics and that was that. I would no more have thought of going out with Tess's brother Bill than of flying to the moon. And the space between us put an awkwardness into any conversation I had with her. I was, in fact, a little afraid of her. She was black-eyed and direct.

Now I think of it, there was a profound division all along that shore. Tess's church, white board-and-batten with a rounded apse that glimmered like a ghost on summer nights, was bigger than ours. Its churchyard bore witness to many more generations of settlement than ours did. The names were French and Irish. And we didn't know any of the French or the Irish except the McCrorys because my father worked with Tess's sometimes; otherwise, Catholics were not available to us. We were like French and English in Montreal, looming invisibly over each others' shoulders.

So my world was a half-world, with Tess and her folk eliminated by historical necessity, and the Indians faint and unknowable also, the mental map of the river shore blurred and half-erased by habit and prejudice. One didn't know the Catholics, or the Indians, or old, foreign people, or the summer cottagers from town, who put more lumber into their fences than into their bedrooms. One knew very little, one walked alone.

Then a funny thing happened; oh, perfectly normal for someone else, but strange for me. Although most summers I had rather grudgingly helped Doog in the store, my parents fixed for me one year to work in the library in Pekin, the village on the river north of us. The library was just a room in Sadie Maislow's house, the township rented it from her the way the post office rents peoples' livingrooms, and Mrs Maislow had fixed it up with a bridge table for a circulating desk and a couple of boxes of file cards and bookshelves. I had never used it much as it contained mostly sentimental novels of the sort Mrs Maislow herself enjoyed – there was a heavy emphasis on "Elizabeth" and "Ouida" – but I was pleased with myself for having the job because Mother was talking about my working in one of the big stores in town and I was terrified of that.

I worked from one to five and seven to nine that summer. Mrs Maislow taught me the cataloguing system, bought me a new stamping pad, and retired to her kitchen. She said she never had anyone half as knowledgeable as me before, and proceeded to make pickles to her heart's content. The memory of the summer is suffused with the smell of vinegar.

She dyed her hair, Sadie Maislow, and wore in it a rough, dark braid around her head. She had a voice like grit.

I bicycled in every day and served my few customers, reorganized the holdings, hoping to find more and better books, and, for my dinner hours, to avoid the vinegar, bicycled along the river shore to sit and watch the lakers go mooing by. I loved the way they bulked and loomed and suddenly filled the whole of the view and disappeared again, and my father had taught me to say, "Ha, she has a bone in her teeth," or "Business is bad, she's going home empty," and I knew which of them carried oil or ore or grain from the Lakehead or the refineries or the iron mines up north, and which companies which smokestacks belonged to. It was before the Seaway, Philip, before industry spread south and polluted the river, before the government organized all the little wastelands on the shore into what they called "parkettes"; one could hide among the willows.

One day I went to my favourite place and there was a man there. I muttered something in embarrassment and went to move away, He looked at me. "The girl from the library!"

"Yes." No one had recognized me before except to accuse me of things.

"Well, don't run away. I was thinking there must be someone around here to talk to."

His name was Boris. He was forty, a schoolteacher in Toronto, and he had come to the shore for the summer to do some writing. He had hoped to find something in that library other than Prisoners of Zenda and Sadie Maislow and he was in luck, he had found me.

I was eighteen and, if I was emotionally retarded, I was still fully grown. It did not take me long to fall in love with Boris. Oh, we talked! After that, in fine weather, we had both our suppers together under the willows, and when it rained he would come to the library for me and, in full view of Sadie M., take me off in his car to his cottage. (I had wanted to sneak but he said it was beneath his dignity.) It was small, had been left him by an aunt, and was stuffed with such things as I had never seen before – real paintings and watercolours, and books, books, books.

He opened a number of worlds for me, Boris; he was a fast education. He had been overseas in the war, to Italy, France, Belgium. He called it sightseeing the hard way. He told me about art, architecture, music. He had long-playing records and taught me to recognize the cadenza in the Fifth Brandenburg Concerto. He was reading Charles Williams that summer and lent me those rich, strange novels whose protagonist is always Faith. He began, a little, to make love to me – here I was a more eager pupil than I had feared I would be and he had to hold me back because he knew about girls, our Boris – he even taught me to drink a little.

Eventually, of course, Sadie Maislow told my parents, and the fat was in the fire. "A Married Man!", my mother shouted ("Now Ellner, now Ellner"). "You sly, wicked wretch!" I sobbed and sobbed. Father went to see Boris. Boris, always a gentleman, came to see me in the library. "The jig's up, kid. Besides, I have to go home. If it gets bad, eat something you can't eat, like cardboard."

I spent the remaining two weeks of the summer glaring at Mrs Maislow who finally said, self-justifyingly, "Well, Rita, I was *told* he was a married man; I didn't know he was divorced. But you know, dear, he was far too sophisticated for you. You ought to stick to your own kind." Which did not help.

At home, I was in deep disgrace and confused as well. They said I had behaved in such a way that they could no longer trust me. "You went to his *house!*" Mother said.

"What's the harm in listening to a few records?"

"As if that was all that was going on!"

And much more. What a relief for mothers now that they can simply put their daughters on the Pill. It was a relief, too, when the sullen summer ended and I began my last year of high school.

My father had never been a well man. He had always made enough to keep us going, but Mother did not press him to earn. She saw herself as a prop, a comforter. He was her eldest child and the one she had most patience with. Therefore, when the guidance teacher at the school called them in (twenty miles there, twenty miles back in the failing Pontiac) and presented them with the idea that I should apply for a scholarship to university, she was furious. She had looked forward to even her ugly duckling's launching into the world. Birds who wouldn't leave the nest had to be shoved, she knew that. She didn't want me staying home like queer Uncle Jake who stayed home with Aunt Kate for twenty years clipping the newspapers and filing the clippings in the encyclopaedia. He was a good forty before they could persuade him to do a hand's turn, and at that he went up to the Yukon and froze to death because he didn't know how to manage.

The problem of what to do with me was not easy to solve, but university was not what she had in mind. Hilda had got on well in university and become a Latin teacher, but it did not look to her as if I had the character to survive in such an environment. Better, she told the guidance teacher and me, for me to take a typing course my last year in school, like Shirley, and work in town and board at Hilda's until I married; or I could go to Normal School, that was only a one-year course, and become a kindergarten teacher. What would I *do* at university?

I looked up shyly and said I wanted to become a philosopher.

Oh dear, poor Mother, what had she done? It must have been, she said, the job last summer, looking after the Pekin Library, and that awful man, that Boris, I went out with, who put such ideas in my head.

The guidance teacher gave me a look, I knew then she knew about Boris. I squirmed guiltily. The guidance teacher shrugged. Girls will be girls, her shoulders said. She went on opening university calendars for a while, then paused, put her pencil behind her ear and said to my mother and father, "It would be good for the school, and good for the county if Rita won a scholarship."

They capitulated. Educating Rita the dreamer might have seemed a dubious proposition, but the school and the county meant something.

*   *   *

Philip, I'm like that bird up there, whirling around the old stories and booming with my wings on the downrush, trying to find a meaning the way he is hunting insects, then getting excited and further and further from the point, forgetting in the end that there *is* a point, spiralling for the feel of the wind. But there must be a point, Philip, a point or a pattern. I wouldn't feel I could go on living if I didn't feel there was a point.

It reminds me of something I perhaps should not tell you that happened last year. Like a lot of women my age here and now, I found myself in a strange motel room with a strange man. It had seemed a good idea when we met, but as I was getting out of the bathtub to go to him I saw myself in the mirror and thought, that is an old woman's body, you cannot walk naked across a room to him wearing that. I smuggled myself into his bed in a towel.

"What're you all wrapped up for?" he asked.

"I'm too old to walk naked in front of a strange man."

"What do you think I expected? You want to be nineteen again?"

We talked all night about James and the Figure in the Carpet. Among other things. Pity I never saw him again.

I'm just past forty, which is not, now, technically considered old. It's a poor age, on the other hand, for encountering strange men when you're in my shape. But he was perfectly right to ask if I wanted to be nineteen, and now, when I think back to the year I went to university, I realize people who are nineteen are, above all and necessarily, greedy.

For I can see my two grey-haired parents sitting before the guidance counsellor. They were aware she might consider them country bumpkins. They wanted to convey their willingness to educate me. They knew they had to do something about me. If by this time no young man had appeared at the door in a four-door Chev to spirit me off, no one would. I would have to be trained to earn a living.

On the other hand, they were both over fifty. They had raised four children with, considering their income, great decency. Most of the food we had ever had on our table had been earned, I think now, not by purchase, but by old-fashioned barter. When my father fixed something for a farmer, he came back with a roast of beef or half a crate of eggs. Flour we got when he did a job for the miller at Binnstown. Cash money crossed their palms irregularly. We did not shop often at Doog's – or anywhere else. If I was to go to university, the money (now that the war was over and the job my father had that was referred to as his *paid* job was also gone) would have to be begged or borrowed. But of course I didn't know that. I hadn't taken it in.

They were not against education. On both sides of the family some of the children, both male and female, had gone to university. My Uncle Stanley was a professor at the University of Toronto. Bob had gone to Western and Ron to the agricultural college at Guelph. There was Auntie Hilda to think of and her degree in Latin, though she only substituted now so I had no way of knowing whether she taught well or not. There was the saying "If you educate a man, you educate an individual; if you educate a woman, you educate a family." But educating me, Rita the dreamer, who, as they said, wouldn't know if she had two left shoes on or not, must have seemed to them exhausting and useless.

As it turned out to be.

However. It was decided. I made out the forms. I got a summer job in town and commuted with Billy McCrory, who was working in the foundry. I worked at the Hydro office, sorting out electric bills, and liked the job. It was like homework, a methodical, set task, and I was good at it. I banked my wages

47

and with the rest bought myself some good functional clothes: a really good navy blue skirt, red, white and blue pullovers, a pair of good oxfords. Clothes for a scholar.

I got the scholarship – none of us had any doubts about that – and, the second week of September, packed my good functional clothes in my father's First World War footlocker and set off for what I had thought would be a good read.

The Sunday before I left the minister prayed for "that one of our congregation who is about to embark on a great voyage." Others came to the house to suggest that there were reefs of worldliness I must avoid. My parents were embarrassed. I was annoyed. I was not going to Oxford or Cambridge or Radcliffe or even McGill (I had privately favoured universities with red calendars but they were all very expensive) but to a small Baptist institution only sixty miles away, where I was sure there would be neither reefs nor shoals. I only hoped there was a good library. While mother watched with a warning half-smile, I knelt and prayed with the ladies of the W.M.S. and the W.I., that through education I should not lose my faith. "Never mind, Mrs Sproule," Mother said to one of them, "Stanley's boy, John, is there. He'll take care of her."

God knows how they paid for me. My scholarship was not large; it covered only fees. In those days, all the students from out of town lived in residences on the campus. If I recall, five hundred dollars was the cost of board and room. My summer money was for books and clothes and personal expenses.

On the way down, Father remarked that Stanley's boy John was really Walter's boy, Millie's youngest, although Stanley had raised him. Perhaps it would be good to remember that.

Mother said suddenly, "I wanted to go to university, too, Rita. It broke my heart when they said they could only send Hilda."

"What would you have studied?"

"Spanish."

Did she long for a land of señoritas? Had she harboured, in her youth, Byronic fantasies? Even I had never thought of Spanish.

Then they discussed what good money teachers were making

now. No mention of philosophy. They didn't know I was going to a temple I was going to be able to ask questions in, having given up on Sunday school teachers and ministers.

Physically and aesthetically the university was, at first, a disappointment. It was smaller than our high school. I was assigned a room in a shabby, old, fake Tudor house with unpainted plaster walls a hundred thousand girls had scratched their names on; Mother and I looked at the plaster. She said, "It was all the rage not to paint once." I said, "I'll miss my tulips." Father and someone else's father brought my trunk up. Then they left me. "Be a good girl, Rita," not, "Have a good time."

There were two beds in the room but my own was the only one occupied that first night.

On the second day I was sent to the gym to register for my courses. I handed my forms to an elderly professor who wielded a university calendar. He asked what course I wished to take. Boldly, "Philosophy."

"Hmmm." Then: "Your scholarship is for Honours English."

"I want to take philosophy."

"You don't have the prerequisites."

"I have a scholarship. I'm smart enough." I felt myself getting bolder.

He held the calendar out with a ridged and horny thumb. "See: trigonometry."

"What for?"

"Logic!" he snapped. "The essence of philosophy is logic! True mathematical logic. You women think it's all the dove of peace brooding over the world, but it's logic! That's why you can't do it. No philosophy for you, my girl, they've got you down for Honours English."

Too late I remembered I had a cousin in the philosophy department. Snap, snap, snap, he had me down for exactly the same courses I had done in grade thirteen, with the addition of religious studies (because it was a religious foundation I was to study at) and, for the sum of forty-eight dollars of my summer pay, elementary philosophy as an extra.

I panted off to the bookstore and went through my list: there were riches in store. I then went back to the women's residence and looked scornful when the dean of women told us collectively that in our dealings with men we were to remember never to come in feeling rumpled. Nobody was going to rumple me.

Courses were to start next day. There were still rituals to be undergone. We wore funny hats because we were freshmen, and were assigned to older students called Big Sisters. Mine was a pinched woman who wore a middy. She was training to be a deaconess in the church, she said. That night, she came in and prayed that I be protected from worldliness.

"I'm not afraid of it," I said.

"You will be," she threatened.

Next morning I found out what she meant. Returning from my first lecture, I found in my room, standing beside a tall, portly man who was, I swear, wearing a morning coat, the most beautiful woman I've ever seen. Her name was Christabel Clavering, and she was to be my roommate. I sat enchanted as she kissed her elegant father good-bye and called him Papa. I watched her unpack her beautiful clothes, even gave over part of my closet to her. Then the buzzer sounded to announce that I had a visitor.

"Oh, let's go and see," she said. "First one's good luck." We rushed down to the front hall and found my cousin John there, Walter's or Stanley's boy, a weedy, weak-eyed, red-headed Heber: the same morning, he and I fell in love with Christabel.

In a way, she took the curse off first year, which continued to be a disappointment. The books were set, very set. The French novel we read painfully, word by word, was the same one we had read the year before in West China. The Latin was, fortunately, Virgil's *Georgics,* which I continue to love, and the English survey course was longer; the history was, again, British nineteenth century, although it was more difficult and one learned about Kitty and Parnell. The philosophy course was elementary, but what I wanted, and from it I learned one valuable thing that had not occurred to me before: every decision, down to choosing the colour of one's shoelaces, was not a moral decision. It had been in our house, but it wasn't here. Like a uniform it simplified my life.

But the largest part of my education that year was Christabel. She was a shock. She had heard that there were moral decisions and dismissed the idea. She knew nothing about the uses of money, the necessity of eating, or obligations of any kind. She was serenely and gloriously independent of rules. She sat down with the Women's Residence Regulations and looked them over with a trained, boarding-school eye.

"Look," she said. "It's simple. We get two late leaves a week. Not enough if we've got anything going. So you take mine and I take yours when we don't need them." We were practising each others' signatures when my Big Sister looked in.

"Don't bother," I waved to her. "I'm all right."

"Does your cousin have a lot of money?" Christabel asked.

"I don't think so."

"He's a professor."

"No, I think he's just a student-teacher. You know, teaching a bit, and finishing his Ph.D."

"He's not very good-looking."

"He has an interesting mind," I said loyally.

"Then we'll have him for interest and the others for fun. Did you buy a College Survey?"

"Yes."

"Good. I'll use yours. Now let's go out and find a restaurant. I told Papa I wasn't going to have one more year of ghastly food and I meant it. We'll eat the College Survey."

She looked like a flower. All the boys envied my living with her and I knew why. She was one of the rare creatures whose beauty is sustained by no artificial aids; she woke as lovely in the morning as she looked all day. She had round grey eyes and lovely teeth and a heavenly smile. Nothing about her was imperfect. When I saw her undressing and thought of her piece by piece I understood, finally, what men saw in women's bodies. Her flesh was fine-textured and blue veins showed through her skin. She was as substantial as any girl of our generation, but beautifully . . . arranged. All her underwear was made of lace.

She was fun, too. She had not a moral in the world. She would groan in pain in the morning and send me over to the

51

dining hall for a breakfast tray because she was ailing. She failed to understand why I could not lie in turn and return the favour. She did not know it was evil to lie; she thought it was evil to be uncomfortable. She hung our room with Japanese prints from home and a little Matisse drawing one of her brothers had sent her from France. She spent a whole week's allowance covering those of our books she considered ugly with flowered wallpaper. When she was bored, she went to the bookstore rather than the library: she liked her books new.

According to my mother's stories, rich girls were always very strictly brought up. Christabel was certainly rich, for her father owned a knitting mill in town and lived, with his second wife, in a grey stone palace above the river. He was a sidesman at the Anglican Cathedral. Her stepmother was from France. But whenever strictness appeared on Christabel's horizon she managed to do exactly what she wanted to. Her mother had died at her birth, she said, and she had had a lot of experience in getting around nannies and housemothers.

The dean of women took me aside and told me I was supposed to be steady, a good influence.

John took us both out for coffee and told us about his thesis. He said it was on metaphysical proofs of the existence of God. I asked him how Uncle Stanley, the atheist, liked it. Christabel questioned him expertly, drawing out his best side. With her, he was almost witty. When he and I were alone he was morose.

All the men wanted to take Christabel out; some of them asked me out to get to her, and if she wasn't using my late leaves, I went. I liked the ones who, unlike rutting country boys trying to roll one in the ditch after Young Peoples', took an interest in the films they took me to see. There were rutting country boys, too, and I lashed out at them with a satisfyingly prurient indignation. Boris had introduced me to the pleasures of *refined* courtship – though that is not what Boris would have called it – and I would settle for no less. Sadly, the ones with the interest in the movies were the ones who waited next time for direct access to Christabel.

Twice that fall I was lectured by the dean of women on how

her purpose in putting me with Christabel was that she should learn my good Christian ways, not that I should go over to hers. And I, who had joined the church by the Laying On of Hands (a ceremony with a great deal of meaning, by the way, when it is performed by the elders of a congregation rather than by a bishop), and therefore had taken on responsibility for my own soul, argued that the fact that Christabel was beautiful did not make her evil, and denied that she was signing my leave card. The dean shook her head. There were witnesses, she said. She gated us both for a week and said that next time we would be up before House Council.

John came over every night that week and we had marvellous discussions of metaphysics.

The university was nothing if not a pious institution. Freshmen were required to go to chapel in the morning, which I enjoyed because of the hymns. They were mostly the same as our own, salvationist in tone, except for Bunyan's "Who Will True Valour" with its hobgoblin (which the new Anglican hymnal has excised: I tell you, Philip!). There were also little moral disquisitions by theology professors which might well have been called sermonettes. They did not seem essentially different from anything I had heard in Heberville, though there seemed to me to be an excessive emphasis on gaining the world and losing one's soul, as if the good professors were *afraid* of running a university.

Christabel never went to chapel. She had one of her boyfriends sign her name on the list that came around.

Funny, that place is a common or garden Ontario university now, financed not by its church, but by government grants. It's enormous, largely devoted to the sciences, and would not recognize itself if I told it its history. There is still a great deal of emphasis on moral philosophy, I am told, but it is no longer the place where, when asked a question about Sartre, the head of philosophy pauses and says, "Oh, the *pagan*."

Christabel was the pagan there. When, at the end of the year, she had seventeen term papers left over to write and I had none, I decided not to envy her her social life: I would regain my scholarship, and she would fail. To my amazement, she shut herself up for a week (sending me back and forth from the library for bundles of books) and wrote them all.

When the year was over, I went home and home seemed humbler, smaller. Mary and Doog has sold the store and moved, outlandishly, to Florida. Mother and Father seemed shrunked and dried, as no doubt they were. It was a hot summer and I commuted to work again with Billy McCrory and haunted the library, half-hoping to find myself a lover between the books. The only consolation was that Billy's sister Tess was home from Brescia Hall, calling herself Treesa. She had decided to major in Irish studies and restore the true dignity of her people. I couldn't, myself, see the dignity of the Great Cattle Raid of Coole, but I loved her stories about the nuns and the prurience. They made my battles with the dean of women and my Big Sister sound like skirmishes.

Tess had grown up to be almost as good-looking as Christabel. She had fine black hair that sprang lively from her head, which she coiled around in a disregard for feather cuts I liked. Her black eyes flashed. When the moon or a name came up, she knew the black side of it. "Tess the Landlord's Daughter," Billy called her when he dropped her off at the creamery where she worked (she claimed there were mice in the vats) and I knew what he meant.

Toward the end of summer I had my one letter ever from Christabel, inviting me to visit her at her parents' cottage up north. This was the subject of much family debate. Finally, we decided that I would lose only part of a week's income if I went in the very last week. Then there was the question of clothes. Loyally, Father thought me right as I was. Mother pointed out the need for white for tennis. My suitcase was packed with great seriousness, as an invitation from the Claverings was not to be either overpraised or sneered at. It contained, in the end, Tessie's white trousers and a bathingsuit mother and I ran up on the old sewing machine with great difficulty.

The journey jerked me farther away than I had ever been. I was ill with worry changing trains in Toronto. Finally, a boy in a yellow convertible met me at Huntsville station. "You for Christabel?" He threw my old case in the back and roared off with a noise that prevented any communication. He raced me over bumpy forest roads, then he stopped with a jerk at a dock. He threw me and my case into a motorboat and roared off towards what seemed either a hotel or a castle. Where we stopped, there were a dozen young people on a raft. They all screamed as he swirled by fast enough to half-tip them. Christabel waved. He took my case up to the verandah and dropped it there, and disappeared. I sat there waiting for Christabel, still miserably travelsick, pretending to be very, very casual. In an hour, she swam off the raft. "Oh," she clapped her hand over her mouth. "I forgot. It was *you*!"

I studied Christabel's friends carefully. Lord knows, since none of them spoke to me, I had the time. I think what they were doing was enjoying themselves, but it was hard to be sure. They leapt about a lot and drank beer. In the evening, they built bonfires and drank martinis and told jokes about excrement, which made everyone giggle.

"For God's sake, Rita, take a drink, it won't kill you," Christabel snarled. But I, who had signed The Pledge and forgotten about Boris, held the beer bottle gingerly and dropped it in little dribbles in the sand. Which I later sat in.

At last, the painful week was over; I went home, packed, and returned to the university. Christabel and I resumed our old relationship. She lived my social life and I supplied textbooks.

There were, however, changes. We both had more freedom, and to my surprise I took advantage of it. I began meeting other readers in the stacks, some of whom took me to coffee and some to dances. And although dances were and are a ridiculous institution, they provided opportunities for both prettiness and propinquity. Christabel gave me one of her evening gowns – she had six – and she and the religious don on our corridor ran up the gussets to make sure its strapless top did not slide off my thin body, and although I attached myself to no one I had what I believe is called a marvellous time.

Christabel meanwhile was seeing both more and less of my cousin John. As a don in the men's residence, he was often engaged in the evenings. But his thesis was at the typist's, and he liked to take her for long afternoon rambles over the hills and valleys of the outskirts of the city. She would come in curiously toffeed with autumn leaves, swearing about having to go out with someone else in the evening.

I said I was a sort of snob, Philip, but I was not ambitious for the sort of life she led. What I suppose I wanted then was a life with the electric quality one finds when extremely good things come together. I was after Keatsian romanticism, not Christabel's baronial home in town, or her martinis in Muskoka. That year I experienced a number of little epiphanies: once when I was reading *Tess of the D'Urbervilles* on a train, an old man sat down beside the pot-bellied stove (they had put the old plush cars back on for the Christmas trade) and started playing "Oh Susannah" on a mouth organ; when in the Politics Club discussion became heated and Carter Williamson laced his foot around mine, I thought for a moment we were roots from the same tree; in a lecture on Chaucer, the leaves around the leaded classroom windows began to rustle in Middle English.

Sounds like a bad version of "Happy Days," doesn't it? It was. The sacred pre-Pill fifties, when Korea was a rehearsal for Viet Nam. Still, some of the times were good, and nearly all the books were. And in second year one had the freedom of the stacks, and the courses were a compensation for all the disappointments of first. One met surrealism, existentialism (in French, if not philosophy), the German Expressionists. One could do ethics instead of St Paul for religious studies. Times were good.

Almost. Besides my own life, I was living Christabel's and John's. He was mesmerized by her and she was at least impressed by the intensity of his feelings. He had virtually no money, but he managed to bring her small presents, like a squirrel scurrying to her with nuts and seeds. She was entranced by his meagre courtship. It would have been a lovely romance if the three of us hadn't had just one brain we passed around like the eye of the fates or the Norns.

Thus in February, in the thick of second term, Christabel began to throw up a lot. She cried, and confessed to the two of us that she was pregnant. We came up with the brilliant idea that she and John should marry. (It was a calamitously naive idea, but one had such ideas then. There were no alternatives. I don't think I had ever heard of the term "abortion" and besides, if girls got pregnant then, they got married. I don't know why I, who was so censorious of others, decided that it was all right for Christabel to have broken Rule Number One of our morality (thou shalt not go all the way), but either I accepted it as a fact and forgot about it, or else I decided it was good for Christabel, who was rich and beautiful, to do the things that the poor and less-favoured had not the courage to do. At any rate, I have never defended anyone, even myself, as hard as I defended Christabel that year, and much good it did me.)

It wasn't a joyous wedding. It was held discreetly in the chapel of the Anglican cathedral. The person who officiated wore a surplice with frilly cuffs. The dean of women, who attended without being asked, looked disapproving. Uncle Stanley from Toronto was a dour best man. Christabel's father, in a pearl grey morning coat, looked exactly as a capitalist should when he is handing his daughter to the nephew of Dr Stanley Macrae, Marxist economist, friend of J.S. Woodsworth, and husband of a leading Toronto Trotskyite. Neither Aunt Frieda, the Trot, nor Christabel's stepmother bothered to attend. Christabel and I wore our best suits, New Look, right down to our ankles, and carnation corsages, all John could afford. She looked haggard and I distinguished myself, while they were signing the register, by fainting dead away. I got a new start in life even before they did.

I remember nothing between the witnessing of their signatures and waking up in my bed at home. Dr Stern and I often talked of this evasion, but I could never summon up its entire content. It had something to do with the way I felt about the lives of women; obviously also some jealousy of Christabel; equally obviously a large portion of a growing fear of sex – in those days one was damned if one did, damned if one didn't, and I have always wanted to have things both ways – but I think it also contained a prophetic quality. I suddenly saw, I remember my knees saw as they crumbled, that the marriage would be a disaster – and perhaps that most marriages are disasters – and arranged with my consciousness to absent myself from the pain of this vision.

So that while Christabel and John went off on a subsidized and miserable honeymoon to stormbound Bermuda, I began an episode in my life that was truly lyrical and led to many strange things.

My mother, a practical woman when she was not confronted by definitions of sexuality, and a great riser to occasions, seemed glad to have me home. I was a patient, something concrete she could deal with. My father, besides, was in a fairly healthy stage and working at a factory in town, no doubt to pay for my education, and out all day. That spring came early. For days, she cosseted me, running trays up and down the stairs to my sunny room without a hint of martyrdom, running after me with cardigans when I was well enough to walk outside, making sure I had the books I needed, sometimes and, I think, with enjoyment, reading aloud to me. She was quite wonderful and we were close, and I loved her.

My room was on the south side of the house and the wallpaper had tulips on it, in regular bunches scudding diagonally from floor to ceiling. The windowsills were deep. Aunt Mary laughed at our brown tin beds, but the mattresses were good, and with enough goose-down pillows your back was shielded from the cold metal as you read. It was a sunny room. I had no dressing table, but a solid maple dresser from Grammacrae's with big honest knobs to the drawers. Mother often debated painting it white, but could not, fortunately, bring herself to do so. Since I had become studious and was the last child at home, I had been given a big oak study table with twisted legs and end panels filled in with knotted wicker or gut like a tennis racket, and a good heavy gooseneck lamp. And brass bookends with Lindbergh on them.

From this sunny room, it had been decided (Mother herself had descended on the dean of women), I would finish my year's course myself. My father was able to procure most of the books I had to read from the library in town, and when I was really well again, they decided, I was to go to old Mr Laidlaw up the river for tutoring, so that instead of writing spring examinations I could write August supplementaries and, if I did well enough, retain my scholarship and return to finish my degree.

There was some sacrifice involved. Indeed, Mother once showed me the bank-loan notes the program required. Mr Laidlaw, of course, must be paid – he looked as if he lived on air but he was a retired Anglican clergyman and must have his toast and tea. In addition, there was the loss of income from my summer job. But there was no word of my leaving the university, for Hebers never quit. Even poor benighted John was staying on at the university, finishing his lecturing. Christabel, of course, would stay in their apartment, for it would not be decent to allow her to parade her condition around the campus. I wondered briefly if she would be asked to join the Faculty Wives' Club, smiled, and took up my books.

Oh, Philip, I am a lazy woman; all I need is a bit of sun, a comfortable bed, and books. It was a lovely spring, and when my body stopped acting out my soul's rebellion (our doctor sometimes came to take my pulse but never said what I had had so I presumed it was something out of a novel, like brain fever) and Dad greased up our old (female) bicycle, I wobbled up the washboardy road and then up the highway to old Mr Laidlaw's with joy in my heart.

He was a serene old man who lived in a house I had often noticed, a wide-fronted building with the name WALLINGFORD in large letters on the eaves of its verandah. He seemed as tall and lean as William Wordsworth, but his cheeks were very

59

pink. He had, like all the people on the shore who lived in named houses (aside from summer cottages called Dunrovin and The Crows' Nest) come from England.

He had been a curate in Somerset. He had also had something to do with, curiously, a Church of England congregation in Buenos Aires, and had come here twenty years ago to live with his sister, the widow of an English doctor who had been a great character on our shore, though he never doctored any of us because we, of course, were United.

I had heard of Mr Laidlaw before, because I had known people who had come to him for tutoring in Latin in high school. He had given Greek lessons, too, to Asher Bowen, whose parents lived further up, on the river side of the road, in the big white house obsured by a wood planted with daffodils.

Old Mr Laidlaw knew his poetry, knew his verse, distinguished between the two, and disapproved of W.H. Auden. But had met Bridges! And was superb on T.S. Eliot.

What a term it was! We did *Middlemarch* together, *The Golden Bowl* and *To The Lighthouse*, though he never converted me to Trollope. We did Chaucer, which brought out a kind of learned sweetness in him, so that if I think of the "Parlement of Fowles" I feel the soft grey cut-velvet cloth on his study table. We read Coleridge, we read Wordsworth, and particularly we read Donne, Herbert, Vaughan, Crashaw. And Hopkins.

The sun burned and the summer whirled in a ball before me. I was lost in a metaphysic of love, the shore was metamorphosed. Toadflax and chicory turned to banks of violets, the dry Canadian trees plumped out to English lushness, the people I saw transformed themselves to portraits by Nicholas Hilliard. Even the stocky Indians and their dry, lean dogs became, if not noble savages, symbols of injured innocence. My heart was tender.

My parents were not surprised when I took to going to Mr Laidlaw's church. It was the one my cousin Betty used to save her nylons in. If the Anglicans were not workers or even givers (would Our Church have left Mr Laidlaw in such a plight?)

they were still Christians, Protestants even, in spite of their creed with its small-c catholic in it, and I was healthy, I had colour. "Your eyes are shining, now," my mother said with a smile, and seemed to plump out, too.

I went first to Mr Laidlaw's church for the language, as many students of English literature do. It seemed sane and dignified and, above all, stately; the hymns had no salvationist gore in them; it sanctified the saints. It was the place I belonged in, as a student of English literature. Mr Laidlaw, though he was not the rector, had taken the charge for the summer, and preached fine, dry, formal sermons with phrases cribbed from Crashaw and Donne, which he and I recognized; so it all seemed for me.

I went to him three times a week, and the rest of the time thumped out papers and exercises (Mr Laidlaw believed that one learned prosody best by writing parodies) on Uncle Doog's discarded Underwood typewriter, or studied the complicated questions of ancient and modern verse or how George Eliot and Virginia Woolf handled time differently, and failed to appreciate H.G. Wells. (Arnold Bennett, of course, seemed to have written straight from home.) I was as happily occupied as a human being can be.

One Saturday in July Mr Laidlaw invited me to drive up to London, Ontario, with him and visit a friend who would be better able than he was to discuss with me Herbert's concept of grace.

He had an old '46 Chev that he drove at at least thirty miles an hour. The upholstery was itchy on my summer legs. It seemed a little too intimate to be sitting next to him in the front seat of a car but I had put on white gloves.

As we drove into London, he began to sing "For All the Saints" in a tiny, high, little voice like a bumblebee's. "You will be most interested in my friends," he said.

Oh, Philip, profit and loss and living and who and what are we? But I was happy, once, that summer, and I am happy almost in that same simple way this summer, and there have been other times, winters even, and I must be grateful for what

61

I have. And isn't it odd how it has been given to me so often to be one of the lilies of the field?

Often enough I've felt like poor old Stirling the starling, the one I watch teetering on the wire here outside every morning, afraid to fly, and belly-flopping off at the last moment when he's so hungry he could cry. And I've stood, too, like the herons, on one cold foot, waiting in the grey dawn, waiting for what will keep me alive.

But I've soared as well, like my goofy windhover. I'm a lucky woman, Philip, though not what you think I am.

"You will be interested in my friends," said Mr Laidlaw with his little prim English smile. "They call themselves the Eglantine Sisters."

For a moment I saw a kind of Chaucerian tap-dancing act in my mind. "Nuns?" I asked feebly. "Are they nuns?"

"They are indeed," he said. "They are sisters of the Church of England, and I am their confessor."

The little mediaeval frieze of prettily cloaked sisters wound its way through my mind again. "I didn't know," I croaked, "that there were Anglican nuns. I mean, Henry the Eighth and all that . . . the dissolution of the monasteries."

"Ah, Rita, but remember the period we have been studying. Dr Pusey. The Oxford Movement. Mr Newman."

I rolled the idea around in my head for a little while. We were in London, the flat capital of the western half of the province. There's a funny generosity about London; all the building lots are twice as wide as they are anywhere else.

"They seem a little . . . exotic . . . for London," I said to Mr Laidlaw.

He smiled again. "They are not exotic in themselves, Rita. Indeed, the lives they lead are very plain. But it is true that they have always been considered an oddity here. In fact, the late Bishop Hellmuth, to whom we owe the foundation of the university, quite forbade Miss Isbister, the foundress, to have anything to do with such papist ideas. He was, as you may or may not know, a former rabbinical student, a flower of the Society for the Conversion of the Jews, thus inclined towards

62

the evangelical side of the church. He could not, of course, forbid Miss Isbister to invite six or seven other ladies to live with her."

It's wonderful, isn't it, Philip, the way time makes sense of history? Now that I have read all the books and records you have sent me, and after ten years as part of that elegant pseudo-mediaeval frieze in my mind (and it was like a frieze, Asher always said it was impossible to discriminate among the sisters from the way I spoke of them and I realize now it was because the stylization of their lives – which is essentially what living to a Rule is – removed their individuality. They had habits, so to speak, but no real characters) I can see them almost steadily and whole. I can see Miss Harriet Isbister arguing with the Bishop about her Order, and I can see, now, too late, why that Order attracted me, why it attracted its handful of Victorian and Georgian ladies. We did not then talk, of course, of the search for alternative lifestyles, we were seeing our Victorian ancestors through the contemptuous haze of Lytton Strachey and the artificial romance of *Washington Square* and *The Barretts of Wimpole Street.* I thought I had read everything, as one does think at twenty, but I did not then know that Florence Nightingale had had to take to her bed to escape the social demands of her mother and gain the leisure to invent statistics. If the Puseyites had not reinvented the Orders, someone else would have. And for me, steeped in Eliot and Hopkins, Donne, Herbert, and the spiritual detective stories of Charles Williams, me frightened by the flapping wings of Eros over Christabel, the Eglantines were another epiphany.

The front door of their big Italianate villa was thick, beautifully painted and varnished. It had a substantial brass knocker. Mr Laidlaw reached up to make it tap and Sister Mary Rose opened the door herself, a funny, dry little woman wearing round spectacles and a full-skirted navy-blue dress. She wore her colourless hair in a dry, thin, braid around her head.

"Oh, the good Father," she exclaimed, raising the palms of

63

her hands and smiling a glad wide smile. "And you have brought your friend. Come in, come in. Just this once we shall have tea before confession."

Eglantine House was easily, aside from Christabel's father's mansion, the grandest building I had been in. It was, I suppose, austere for a Victorian; but when I read later of the founding of the First English Order, the Park Village Sisters, and of the simplicity in which those first nuns were expected to live, I am afraid I laughed. Poor ladies, I thought, deserted by the cacaphony of Victorian interior decoration, bereft of birds and shells under belljars, knobs and fobs and funeral wreaths, all those layers of God knows what they had to wear under their clothing, all those ritual morning calls and evening dinner parties; all that tinkling on the pianola that left so many of us with sulky music lessons to get through. Poor ladies, escaping into a life that was Shaker plain. How they must have loved it.

The house was plain, and beautiful in its plainness. The only item of decoration in the front hall was the painting of Sister Harriet. The chairs were hard (but a greater mortification of the flesh, I discover in middle age, is a low, soft armchair), but it was as clean as it could be scrubbed, and it was clear that here discipline was no handful of knotted cords. Compared to the farmhouses of my childhood, it was a sonnet; and compared to my mother and her sisters, who lived in a perpetual struggle against mice, mud, illness, poverty, and the fear of going down, not up in the world, the sisters led lives of ease.

Discipline was a modicum of orange juice in the morning whether you wanted or not. The body was treated as a kind of nuisance, like a two-year-old who must not be spoiled but must be cared for sufficiently to quiet its roarings: a dirty head would itch and spoil one's prayers, a hair shirt make one all too conscious of the flesh. Our underlinen really was linen, Philip, handstitched out of the finest pillowcase material; it was the most comfortable I have ever worn, silky against the skin without being sensuous. Grammacrae could not have instituted a more sensible establishment than Eglantine House, and the Church of Rome would not have understood it. To your friend,

R. Heber, whose life had always been a quest for simplifications, patterns, stylizations, it was peace and bliss.

Would my life not have been completely different if Sister Harriet Isbister had left a few nasty urns around? You're barking up the wrong tree, Philip Huron. It wasn't faith that got me to the nunnery, it was taste.

I went into the hall with Mr Laidlaw and Sister Mary Rose. Sister Harriet's portrait, austerely black-framed, was the only decoration until suddenly and very quietly a young woman with short black hair appeared with a bouquet of sprawling briar roses.

"We allow ourselves our thorny pleasures," Sister Mary Rose said, bowing us into her office. "Sister Cicely, we shall have our tea in half an hour."

Sister Cicely was not attractive. She had a black moustache and black eyes and black short hair. She was my age. She looked at me and didn't like me. She hurried out again silently. She was wearing slippers of black felt. "Sister Cicely prefers to be silent," Sister Mary Rose said.

We sat in two straight chairs by her desk. "We do not cross our legs," she said. "It is a foolish rule, but one we adhere to for the sake of the older sisters, who find change hard to accept. Father Laidlaw has been telling me of your interest in devotional literature, Miss Heber."

I muttered something about exams.

"Perhaps if it lasts, we will see more of you. Usually, Father Laidlaw confesses us before tea, but since you are here, let us tour the building, have our tea, and while we are occupied, leave you reading." She was serenely unanswerable.

From what Mr Laidlaw had said I realized that the Eglantines were different from a Roman Catholic Order. Later I discovered as you did, Philip, that they were different from any other in existence. Sister Harriet Isbister was a plain, sensible woman who had had her wits about her when she set the Order up, and knew well that she had to steer between the Scylla and Charybdis of Protestant bigotry and Papist seduction. Just as she avoided mortification of the flesh in favour of what I can only call de-emphasization of the flesh, thereby reducing the importance of chastity – for how could a plain, ordinary Eglantine, not chafed by her costume, be aware enough of her flesh to exercise its longings? – she and her successors had reduced the importance of obedience by insisting that the Order be run along plain and kindly lines. The Sister Superior was head of the house by consent of its members, and she retained her office by means of her goodness of heart. Sister Mary Rose had authority but I was always aware that she retained it not by means of its exercise, but by her goodness of heart. And the authority she had was no Brownie award for the avoidance of men and mean thoughts. Although I cannot imagine that she ever had an overtly sexual thought in her life (like everyone else I have difficulty imagining my parents, physical or spiritual, engaged in sexual practices) I was never under the impression that Sister Mary Rose had not been severely tempted in other ways; she had won her redemption by strength of character, with the assistance, of course, of grace.

Funny, grace is a what . . . thing, quality, experience . . . which I have never understood outside her office, Philip. All my life people have been sending me off to be educated here and there, as if there were some hole in me they thought the professor could fill up. But it wasn't an intellectual hole. I could always pass an examination in the Structuralism of Religion. But try me on understanding concepts like grace, like love. True understanding, I suppose, is achieved by living through an idea, not just mastering it on the page, and I'm not very good at living. It's taken me most of my life to incorporate its first five years.

Perhaps that is what attracted me to Eglantine House; I sensed in my first visit there that there was something beyond my grasp, something that flitted in and out of my consciousness like a moonbeam, a firefly, or a broken rainbow on a hall carpet that might be there possessed; and it was indeed in Mary Rose's office that I sometimes, fragmentarily, understood that firefly – love, grace, understanding itself; and then I was happy.

66

That first visit there is now intermingled in my memory with nearly ten years in the house, and hard to sort out from them. I remember now only the smell of roses, the smell of furniture polish; the strangeness of the desiccated sisters at tea; the instinctive and disquieting hostility of Mary Cicely (some things are sent to try us), the sweet piety of Father Laidlaw, and, above all, the radiant graciousness of Miss Isbister's cloister.

You said, Philip, of the cloister, "Ah, it takes me back!" And it does, doesn't it? But where? What struck me on that first visit was that the front hall was obviously one's kind, well-off maiden aunt's; the parlour had a hint of Sunday school or church parlour; but the cloister. . .wasn't it a kind of never-never land? By dreams of England out of Browning? I can, in fact, imagine a generation's being annoyed by that cloister, because of its connection with another's Europe-hauntedness, but I find even in its memory some attractive duplicity. I can see Miss Isbister travelling through Italy with her elegantly disguised potato-merchant father saying, "Ah, Papa, what a beautiful column!" and convincing him that the whole dozen little granite pillars with limestone Ionic capitals would be just the thing for a loggia in the garden at home; and afterwards, that they could make a lovely sheltered walk if the wall were extended just here, just there. Other more sinister minds could imagine her plotting, waiting upon his dying, but I have read in her daybooks that statement, "If I covet my father's house, it is for the work of the Lord," and believed it. She was patient and good, if not handsome, Miss Harriet Isbister, and in due course her father did die, but as near to ninety as makes no difference, and she was by his bedside; it was not until that moment that she quietly assembled her spiritual kind and put them to the work of the Lord.

What, of course, the work of the Lord is changes with every generation. The English upper classes seem for a very long time to have interpreted it as the work of the lord and master of the house, a tradition that has lingered to many women's rue in Canada. And mothers have interpreted Lordship as the rule of their sons, and sons have taken this role without asking; and society has often decided the work of the Lord is breeding, not breeding, recycling bottles, or salvaging newsprint. It is frustratingly unclear.

In an England lacking in either freedom for women or social services, the first Anglican sisterhoods decided that the work of the Lord was social work. Nursing and the redemption of prostitutes (a Victorian preoccupation that has not succeeded in crossing time and our space) fell to the lot of the Sellonites and the Park Village Sisters. I gather from Miss Isbister's diaries that it was difficult to convince churchmen in London, Ontario, that the Eglantine Sisters were fit for this work. In fact, the churchmen of London, Ontario, including Bishop Hellmuth, could see no respectable function for the Eglantine Sisters at all. It suited them very well to have Canadian women as hewers of wood and drawers of water – in fact, I think for about two hundred years the owners of this colony thought of it as a home for a peasantry consoled by the possible ownership of their own land, that only – and the idea of a gaggle of spinsters constituting themselves as nuns, withdrawn from the world, from the new world, even, was anathema. Bishop Hellmuth and his elders could not prevent Sister Harriet Isbister inviting a few friends to live with her in her house, but he could prevent them from forming a formal Order, he could prevent their celebrating the Mass in their own house, and he could prevent them from parading the streets of the new London in garments offensive to evangelical taste; and he did. He also suggested, Sister Harriet records, that the poor of the diocese were not in need of spiritual assistance from untrained, addled women as much as of warm knitted stockings. Whereby Eglantine House just failed to become a knitting factory.

He was a good man, Bishop Hellmuth, but on the side of the Evangelicals. He was right, on the whole. He fought to prevent the Church of England from becoming so elitist that the Methodists and the Presbyterians acquired total spiritual power over his diocese. One can only approve of him. The Oxford Movement was not what western Ontario needed. Eglantine House was not a cog in his political wheel.

What it was not, was many other things as well. The Eglantines never did become a full-fledged Order with imperial aspirations; they never acquired an orphanage or a proper school. Miss Isbister and her colleagues were reduced – by Hellmuth and succeeding bishops' disapprobation of almost every positive move on their part – to becoming a contemplative order. And this they did, it seems to me, with grace. They contemplated God, they were orderly, they performed small parish services, they were confessed whenever they could find a curate pale and goitrous enough to be safely asked if he were High Church, they were lovely and full of grace.

When I told my mother that I wanted to join the Order, I discovered to what degree the Eglantines were caught in the cleft of the industrious Canadian stick. God knows what our ancestors thought that they wanted out of Canada except money, land and fur, but by the time Miss Harriet Isbister and I appeared on the horizons of Canada West, the general populace had succeeded in convincing itself that the ideal for womanhood was not Mary but Martha; this was to be a country for workers and those who were not workers were beyond the pale. To withdraw from the world to contemplate one's spiritual heritage was to be an irritant, not a worker but a shirker; it was not taken into account either by the Bishop or or my mother that the Eglantines would gladly have been workers if they had been allowed. The Bishop can be excused on account of his place in history; my mother, of course, knew I was copping out again.

I had my tea, I read in Sister Mary Rose's office while Mr Laidlaw was confessing the sisters, and I decided to spend the rest of my life in that house. I went back to my shore and Mr Laidlaw's velvety drawing room and the poets. On many succeeding Saturdays I drove up to London with him for confessional tea. I also did a good deal of hard talking with Sister Mary Rose, for I had found someone who would take in earnest my questions in the temple. By the end of the summer I was sure of my vocation and I told her so.

She warned me that the way was difficult. I, of course, en-
visaged many spiritual difficulties – it was not going to be
easy to create for myself a crystalline soul – but that was not
entirely what she meant, for when, after I had successfully
completed my examinations and quietly been received into
the Church of England by Father Laidlaw, I announced that
my eventual destination in life was not the Ontario College of
Education but Eglantine House, what can only be described
as "ructions" broke out.

By now I was used to the idea that I could not, except
when I was ill and passive, please my mother. I had even
decided that there would be ructions; but ructions like these I
had never seen before.

I was a liar, a cheat, a thief. I had taken their money for my
education and thrown it away, I had cheated the dean of
women and the whole family by abetting that Christabel in
her seduction of John, I had lied when I said I was going shopping in London with Mr Laidlaw (I had not said I was going
going shopping, I said I was going to see friends of his), I was
a hypocrite if I thought I was religious, what I was doing was
getting out of doing any work, women's work especially, that
I had always been slack at, I was running away, I was failing
to provide grandchildren, I was hiding from the fact that I
had no friends and nobody liked me and I was wasting my
life.

The words in their exactitude I do not remember any more,
but I remember the anger and it makes me shudder still. I picture her with the cleaver held over my head, whereas in fact
the ructions took place in the livingroom, and she had the
darning stick in her hand, jabbing the needle viciously into
Dad's socks (she was right, I never helped to mend) and once
into her thumb, cursing, then rising and shaking her head and
denouncing me again, again, again. "Now Ellner," my father
said, but it did not calm her; and he started coughing and she
said I was killing him and I said I was hardly responsible for
what the Germans did in the trenches in nineteen-ought-
eighteen, and she threw the darning egg at me, and started to
scream and fell down in a kind of fit.

I don't want to go on and on about my mother, Philip, for Dr Stern and I talked about her at length; it didn't seem to him that for the purposes of therapy there was much use talking about relationships that were dead and gone, but of course at that point all my relationships were dead and gone, and so we talked about Mother a bit; I was able at last to reconcile myself to some of her goings-on, though not always, as Sister Mary Rose had pointed out, to forgive her, I suppose because in a way she was for me a kind of negative seeress. If we subtract her bigotry, which was only part of her culture, from her attitude to the Eglantines, she was right: I was escaping the world by joining the Order, and I was wasting my parents' money and I would eventually pay for these sins. And although her hysteria only deepened my resolve to become an Eglantine (and the way to the Order was thorny as it was meant to be – there is a kind of virgin one becomes only with difficulty), her prediction of eventual disaster was true, as it had been when she scolded Stu for his marriage, and Shirl for her painted nails, and me for my teenage manlessness: they were all conditions which led to unsuitable futures.

She did not consciously mean to be a Cassandra, but I doubt she could help it. I think now that she was a difficult woman because she had had a difficult life. She was less clever than some of her sisters and less attractive than others. Her utilitarian view of life (the money she spent on patent corn-removers and utilitarian corsets might have been spent on frivolities for all the help they were to her: she could have had pretty hats and cosmetics and teach-yourself-Spanish records if she had just one year neglected the outside paint or eavestroughing and I often wish now she had never sent me to university) cut her off from any sense that that which was not useful (and certainly Eglantinism is not, to people of my mother's cast of mind, useful) could be beautiful. Marriage was a serious affair meant for keeping peoples' noses to the grindstone; and sex, it seemed to me from the books she gave me about it, was for the martyrdom of women (if you wanted to have to do with it without conceiving, you had first to imagine yourself as made of tubes and pipes, not of petals like a rose: one view is fatal to eroticism, the other to zero population growth, and we haven't yet really solved that one), and woman's role was to take care of men and children. If one became a teacher and instructed them, instead of a mother baking for them, that was acceptable. But she foresaw disaster in the lives we had all chosen, and thought it correct to plant suspicion in our joy.

It does not do to blame. We are our own creatures as well as God's, no matter what the theologians said. Roses and pipes are neither of them the whole story. But I wish she had been a happier woman.

In the end, Sister Mary Rose drove down in the old Eglantine Ford to see my parents, and an arrangement was made. I was to finish university – a degree would be useful to the Eglantines as well as to me, Mary Rose told them, as a teaching sister was needed – and work a year to repay my parents. And if at the end of that year I still wanted to join the Order I would be free to do so. Mary Rose agreed also that I was to stay away from the convent for that year, so that they could not consider me seduced. In return, they said they would prefer me to take a simple, three-year pass degree, which would save some expense. Thus Sister Mary Rose would get her teacher, but not a first-class one, and they would be able to retire a year earlier.

I agreed privately with Sister Mary Rose to pray to God for grace to love my mother better.

I expected that last year at university to be unhappy. Indeed, I made it as austere as I could, wearing the plainest of clothes and rising early to attend matins in a very high Anglican church at the other end of town. But somehow joy kept creeping in, and I suppose now that I wasn't automatically bracketed with Christabel (who had had a wretched screaming baby who looked not at all like John) I had some social currency in myself. Since I went home for weekends very seldom, I made new friends. Even, to my surprise, developed a romance with a boy that I now know loved me, though he was quiet about it. He took me to movies and bought me sandwichy suppers and talked politics with me; he had no money for dances and flowers. He was Jewish and could see my Anglicanism only through Donne and Eliot as a kind of poetry, which of course it was. Sometimes he came to church with me for the music but in the end he confessed that he could see communion only as a kind of cannibalism, and he joked that since I didn't know left from right I'd never make a Jewish wife, I'd mix up the plates for milk and meat, so that was that. But we were fond of each other, and once, with the help of Mozart, we almost made love. I think of him fondly now, for though we agreed to disagree, there was no torment between us, and that has seldom been my arrangement with a man.

I took my pass degree with high marks, a condition I seemed helpless to avoid, and got the first job I could, as a clerk in the Hydro office in Toronto. My mother had kept careful account of what I owed for my education. By buying no new clothes – which meant, virtually, wearing a habit – and eating as little as possible and going nowhere, seeing no one, I paid all that I owed them in that one year.

I was a wraith with a black suitcase when I appeared at Sister Mary Rose's door. She said, "Oh, my dear!"

I do not now think that she thought I was a suitable candidate for the Order. We had many long talks in her office and the substance of her conversation seems now to me to have been discouraging. But I had made up my mind that for God, Harry, and St. George I would be an Eglantine, and although I spent my year as a novice at teacher's college, in the end she let me take what passed for a vow.

And so began the happiest and most innocent ten years of my life.

"Innocent," I can hear my mother and Grammacrae shouting, "Crazy!" And I suppose we were crazy, shut away from the world, more shut away actually than we wanted to be, because the city of London never did get used to us so we held onto the old policy of discretion, even departing for Eucharist at St Thomas's in scattered twos and discreet threes, wearing not veils but conventional black or navy blue hats which we selected with just a hint of malice from Eaton's catalogue

73

whenever we needed new ones. Yes, Mama, we were innocent; far too innocent for your purposes, for you thought it frivolous to attempt to see life as a bed of roses, and frivolity to you was never innocent.

"Innocent!" I hear you snort and I think of Sister Mary Benedicta in the kitchen, bland and dough-faced, at her scouring. She was our cook: she liked cooking. Sister Mary Rose admitted that her theological weakness was that she could not see the point of certain forms of mortification. If Sister Mary Benedicta performed her religious duties well and was attached to cooking, let her cook: though we all took a hand when we were needed.

Sister Mary Agnes did the inside garden, which she had laid out in little bricked squares, some for chives and some for rosemary, some for parsley, some for basil and even celery; against the south wall of the cloister she had managed to espalier some pears, which every other year provided us with heavy-scented fruit. The more utilitarian vegetables she had hidden behind borders of phlox and forget-me-nots. Sister Mary Cicely helped her with this and had a fine hand for both cabbages and roses. And it was she who worked the big vegetable garden to the north, beyond the walls, on the other side of the conservatory. She had been born on a farm and she had no fear of putting her foot to a spade.

I took a long time to get used to Mary Cicely and her moustache (what a shocking thing that we are all so prejudiced against women with facial hair!) though I got used to what I took at first to be her hostility. It took her even longer to accept me, because she had been one of their orphans, the only one who had stayed, and she had a special status among them, she was their baby, the only one under fifty: I threatened her position.

I remember when I met you, Philip, at Maggie Hibbert's dinner party, when I was pregnant, and Maggie had put me beside you because some of the other guests, she said, would be intimidated by you. I had no idea you were The Bishop. When she phoned me she said, "Would you mind sitting beside Philip

Yurn?" I didn't mind anything in those days, for the world, as represented by dinner parties at the Hibberts, was all shining and new for me, and I was pleased, too, with my big childful belly, and smug. And how amused we both were when we found out *who* we were, because you had been winding up the books of the Order, and you found out I was Mary Pelagia.

It was part of leaving the world, of course, to take a new name for a new life. I suppose that was why, when I married him, Asher began to call me Peggy. But I remember best the smile on your face at the party, when Phoebe was leaning over us, trying to look like a sprite or a cherub, pouring out Chilean wine, and you turned to me over her draperies (she looked like a Turkish tart, poor child) and said, "Cicely, Gertrude, Magdalen?" and I nodded.

William Morris would indeed have been pleased with the Eglantines and I can't think God himself wasn't, at that time. I have read, since, books and stories by women who have dropped the veils of the Sisters of St Joseph, of the Ursulines – indeed, there must be dozens of them. But none of them seems to have found the earthly paradise I found for a while in Eglantine House, in London, Ont., as we call it, the heart of your diocese.

Mary Cicely and Mary Agnes the garden; Mary Benedicta the kitchen; Mary Rose, our head and heart. Mary Flora was very, very old, and tottered about, fussing a little, the only one who did so, if she was not allowed her tea on time or her special cup. Mary Dorothy and Mary Beatrice did exquisite embroidery and brought income to the convent by making copes and vestments and giving classes in smocking; Mary Elzevir was a problem, she had attached herself to Mary Rose as a passionate ADC, and guarded her fiercely, and they called me Mary Pelagia.

Pelagia, Pelagia, down by the shore. . . . There should be a nursery rhyme for that, something like "Grace, Grace, dressed in lace," or "One, two, three a-lairy . . ." Pelagia, Pelagia, scudding along the tide-line pretending she is a bird, a plane. Pelagia standing, Pelagia sitting, Pelagia dishevelled from doing handstands on sandbars, Pelagia like Uncle Jim in the bathtub, swimming against the tide. You needn't think of me working all the time, Philip, I'm very busy, very busy wasting time. Becoming, in fact, a child again.

Hard ropes of wet sand under my feet.

Clam digging, high tide: mud sucks the feet, down, down, oozes over into the rubber boots like ribbons of cold snails.

Eating the things: God help us, what are the crunchy bits?

Dr Stern, my rubicund heathen psychiatrist, would be proud of me. "What shall I dooooo?" I used to snuffle at him, "What will become of me?"

He would fix me with a liquid, mournful eye. "Now Rita, now Rita." Then make a house out of his fingers on his fat belly. Which always made me smile. "Do what you want, child, do what you want."

Now I do what I want. Hurl myself like a madwoman against the shallow waves. Bounce across sandbars. Play. For twenty years I've had no time to play. Today my ears are full of water, my hair is full of salt. My tan is crusted with white. I came up out of the water in a clamshell, Philip. Shall I sit five minutes more in the sun, Philip, or go inside into the dim light and pound out "Ein Fester Burg" on the pump organ?

You know, on summer evenings we used to sit out in the cloister stitching at that underlinen that was finer than silk. Mary Agnes had taken a vow of silence by my second year, but the others all made mild conversation – it was forbidden to talk about oneself but there were the birds and the flowers – and we sat in a little circle, Elzevir next Mary Rose, Cicely and I uncomfortably together; Dorothy, Beatrice and Benedicta slightly apart, Agnes and Flora silent for different reasons. Eventually Mary Beatrice would say to Mary Rose, "Could Pelagia not give us a little music, Sister?" and Mary Rose would nod and I would go into the chapel, half afraid of breaking its rose-laden silence, and with a long, hooked pole open its upper window so the Bach chorales my cousin Zoe had taught me to play on the harmonium could get out. I never could reach a proper octave so I scanted the left hand and played in sixths, but either they didn't notice or they were very kind. Mary Rose didn't allow sharp tongues, though one felt she had heard them in her life.

While I was playing (holding my breath so I would not spoil the nightingale-soft evening with wrong notes) I knew Mary Dorothy would unpick my smudgy sewing.

Yes, that's the way it was, Philip; as cool and soft as a psychiatric ward. But an undrugged calm, a harmony. An atmosphere not very many people could create. And it was created not by God, but by Mary Rose.

She was over sixty when I first met her. She had come to the Order rather late. She was a diplomat's daughter who had intended to study mediaeval history at the highest level. Alas, her family had lost its money in the Crash, her father's party had lost favour, and in mid-career she was forced to return to a village not unlike Heberville, but closer to London, to resign her parents to an early and humiliating retirement. She had amusing descriptions of trying to convince her mother that it was possible to live without aides-de-camp. When life was nearly impossible for her, she began to associate with the Eglantines and draw strength and patience from them. She witnessed the last days of Harriet Isbister and when she was liberated came to live at the convent, bringing with her a fine library I always had access to. She became sister superior by common consent on the death of Sister Harriet's successor, Sister Mary Monica, in 1944.

The only thing I was ever told about Mary Monica was that she was uncommonly beautiful and refused to be painted or photographed.

Sister Mary Rose had a fine mind, and she ought to have taught. Perhaps she took me in because she needed a student. My naming, Philip, was only the first occasion on which she produced academic irony, for since my name was Marguerite and my birthday suited one of the many St Margarets, she might have called me that; but she chose Pelagia, not, she pointed out, for the Pelagia who was once called Marguerite for her pearls and Marina because she was an inevitable cognate of Aphrodite, but for Pelagius, theologian and heretic, whose work we should study together; he was, she announced, as great a Puritan as I.

Much nonsense has been written about convents and sexuality; of course the absence of sex implies its presence in the strongest terms, and Christian imagery is as well highly sexually charged. For centuries the idea of chastity has invoked the dancing girls of the mind. Pelagia is more interesting than Pelagius who, though a great bishop and above all a great heretic (few non-military reputations have lasted as long as his, few ideas have been as cruelly influential as his that we save ourselves without grace and are damned if we commit a single sin: I wonder they didn't call Ontario after him), was a rather dry stick. Pelagia of Antioch, on the other hand, was an actress who every night processed in splendour past Bishop Nonnus's fledgling church, causing scandal among the Christians. Finally (could she have been losing her figure? Were her pursuers drawing too near?) she sat herself and her splendid pearls at the feet of the Bishop and asked to be converted.

The women of the congregation were suspicious. Her instant conversion did not win their hearts. But Nonnus, having promised to shrive her, kept his word. She became a holy person, and many years later, when an ancient eremite was being laid to rest, a Desert Father of large piety, much visited by troubled young hermits whose control over their starving visions was incomplete, the body was discovered to be female, that of Pelagia, not Pelagius.

It's a lovely story in its obedience to form and the way it controls its temptations: the need to think, in poverty, of luxury, in chastity, of unchastity. It sits well among anti-papist versions of perversions like the story of Maria Monk among the Grey Nuns of Montreal.

Well, here was I, rechristened Pelagia, among the Eglantine nuns of London, Ontario, the first novice (except it seemed for a disastrous woman they were always going to mention and then clamped their teeth together on) in many years. If there was suppressed sexuality in the air, it was channeled into the roses. The rest of our life together was channeled into an unerringly comforting routine and I often thought of the sisters in terms of their roles, like a Welshman: Benedicta the Kitchen, Agnes the Garden, Dorothy and Beatrice the Needlework. . . .

We were very happy. Habit, order and rule gave our lives structure. We had, like other Anglican sisters, taken most of our rules from the Benedictines and softened them to suit ourselves. Much of our time was spent in the little chapel, which had been Mr Isbister's conservatory, where Sister Harriet had had the family Persian carpets laid down, Mary Dorothy and Mary Beatrice had embroidered kneelers and altar cloths, and instead of stations of the cross, little icons of saints surrounded by the flowers of Ontario (St Catherine of Siena with ladyslippers, St Jude among the trilliums . . .), and Mary Rose had hung a white ivory crucifix from Glastonbury. As a chapel, it struck outsiders as very odd with its bits of stained glass here and there, and homemade canvas blinds (white for Easter, green for Trinity) to shut the sun's rays out. But I felt that our prayers really did rise to heaven.

It was too good to be true, of course, but I cannot condemn an institution that cost nobody anything and made nine women happy.

I worked, partially, in the outside world. I wore ordinary navy blue sweaters and skirts and sensible shoes and taught first in a school for retarded children where I discovered that amateur devotion was ineffective, and later within the secondary school system as one of their revolving religious studies people. Mary Rose also enrolled me at the university, where I studied Anglican theology one year, philosophy another, the sociology of religion yet a third. People are always sending me back to university, Philip: I have one of the great unfinished minds.

Each of us had a special life, a special duty; it was Mary Rose's to find what would make us happy and therefore good. In the moments not given to housework or devotion we each had our jobs to do, and although Mary Elzevir was jealous of my access to Mary Rose's library and I often felt that in her black-eyed fanatical attachment to Mary Rose she was ill-wishing me (I was not old enough, Philip, to understand what the war had done to her), we were on the whole very serene.

It was a good life we lived there, and almost as smooth as cream. In time, I, like the others, grew to fear the appearance of another novice; but Mr Laidlaw aged and faded from our lives and no new intruder appeared. I melted into the routine, cheerfully absenting myself to teach and endorsing my paycheck to Mary Rose without a thought of injustice, taking a course a year towards a Master's degree in God knows what, and keeping out of the others' hair. I did my share of the domestic work as well, and without minding it. The year we got the freezer we were happy as a swarm of bees.

The only unhappiness was my relationship with my parents. My mother decided that even if the Order was Anglican, if I was a nun I was no better than a Catholic, and she cut me out of her life. My father wrote me at Christmas in a tidy hand, but was inarticulate. I went back a couple of times to try to convince them I was not beyond the pale, but they had become small and ingrown, unreachable. They wouldn't even give me Shirley's address. They implied things had gone badly for her. They waved me away with withered hands. Kenny dead, their eyes said, things bad for Shirley (was she divorced? Had she run away? They wouldn't say), Stu, you know Stu. When I saw them last I knew I had no family any more, I belonged only to the Eglantines. I prayed for them, but as if for an elderly couple in a children's book illustration. They were no longer the people I had known.

In time, things began also to change at Eglantine House. I received a regular appointment to teach English and religious history at one of the London high schools; though I had not finished my M.A., my course work was taken into account and I brought to Eglantine House a salary I considered scandalously worldly. Which was as well, for the Hospital Insurance Plan had not yet been instituted, and the sisters were beginning to age and fail. In addition, Mr Laidlaw as confessor had been replaced by a tall, fair clergyman with piercing eyes whom I did not feel either suitable or sympathetic. My heart turned to stone when I was near him.

I would have liked to discuss this problem with Sister Mary Rose, but she had her hands full, for Mary Flora was dying, Mary Benedicta was very ill, and Mary Beatrice was being difficult about the food. It hadn't occurred to any of us that Mary Benedicta was an almost sinfully excellent cook until we had to do without her. Then, while I was still fussing about not wanting to confess to our confessor, we discovered that Mary Beatrice's eyesight was going.

Mary Rose always looked flustered then; she needed, I think, a good deal of time alone in order to be at peace with herself. She was a nervous woman. I volunteered to stop teaching and help in the house, but she was adamant; she said they needed my salary. I have found since that that was not true; I doubt it was a conscious lie; it was a rationalization. She wanted at least one of her children to stay in her accustomed place.

You know some of the rest of the story, Philip. It is hard to give up happiness, even the idea of happiness, hard to accept the idea that roses fade. (Every night now I go up to Mac Moan's road before sunset and stand, just stand, among them and say a prayer for all the Marys, even though I say I am not a believer now, while the petals fall.) Mary Flora died peacefully in her cell at the bottom of the garden, where she had summered every year since she came to the house. She was ninety. Mary Benedicta died painfully in the cancer hospital. As Mary Beatrice's eyesight failed, her voice began to quaver through the collects and the psalms. I tried a little to replace the others and was universally rebuffed: Mary Agnes would let me touch nothing in the garden. Mary Dorothy devoted herself now entirely to Mary Beatrice and spoke not a word to the rest of us. Mary Elzevir increased her fanatical protection of Mary Rose, camping outside her office door like a gypsy fortune-teller.

Out of necessity, Mary Cicely and I drew closer to each other. She was a laconic girl but now that she knew I could not cheat her out of her role as baby of the house – all the mothers were going – she began to be friendly to me. Often as not, we were the only two at chapel in the morning, the only two in the kitchen.

We began to talk when I discovered she was a first-class cook. I watched her in fascination whipping up omelettes, slitting and slotting vegetables with a professional cook's knife with an intentness I had never seen before. And there was a savour to the products of her industry that raised them above the level of good home cooking. I asked her if she had learned from Mary Benedicta.

"No," she said with a half-smile, "in France."

"But you were brought up here, in the house."

"Mary Rose wanted me to see more of the world. She sent me to another convent, one in France."

I pieced the story together over the preparation of many meals as I watched and tried to memorize Mary Cicely's preparations; for though I do not denigrate old-fashioned Canadian cooking, Philip – one misses it terribly now it is gone – Mary Cicely, with much the same ingredients as my mother and aunts had used to use, produced something on a higher level. It was from her I learned to make the leek and potato soup you used to like, and the grilled mackerel.

She told me that Sister Mary Rose had taken her aside when she was twenty and told her that she had a friend in France, also an ex-mediaevalist, who was novice-mistress of an Order called the Mendicant Genevièves; and that she had thought about Mary Cicely's education and how narrow it was, since she had lived in the same house with the same women since her mother died. She felt that Mary Cicely ought for a year to make a probably painful remove to another country, to another way of life.

Mary Cicely also admitted that Mary Rose had previously asked her to go to live in the world, but that she was too much afraid.

So, in the end, with much weeping, she allowed herself to be packed off to the Genevièves.

She had hated it, but she had learned a great deal. The Genevièves lived under conditions of austerity she had almost not survived: stone walls that bled damp in winter, she said.

82

Porridge and gruel for their meals. Sandals even in winter. And they were Roman Catholics. Their services were in Latin, held in an old Jesuit chapel where the paintings were all grey and brown, and she always covered with chilblains. When they were not at services they were sent out to the streets to beg. She was an awful beggar. She could hardly get her arm out of her cloak with the bowl. She thought it was wrong, in her heart she thought it was wrong.

The first three months were agony, she said. She could not get her tongue around French and was totally isolated. The other Genevièves treated her as if she was not there. At the end of the third month the Sister Superior called her in to her office and said, "You have suffered enough, my child," and Mary Cicely began to weep. Moments later she realized the statement was in French, and she had understood. She stopped crying and began to listen.

The Sister Superior said she realized that Mary Cicely was there not only on a voyage of the soul, but on a voyage of education. She had therefore arranged that, without neglecting her religious duties (which were few, since she could not be a communicant except at an English church twenty miles away to which she took the tram on Sundays to sit among decayed gentlefolk), she should make herself useful to a number of good women, friends of the Genevièves, who were elderly and in need of domestic help. Most of them were widows of gentlemen or officers, inhabited large properties of great age, and were being forced by the taxation system to lead lives of abomination. Instead of a beggar, Mary Cicely should be a servant of these new poor.

The houses, Mary Cicely said, were wonderful: palaces to her; mansions with huge doorways you could drive a team of horses into (though not Clydesdales, she said wistfully). Mansions with grand sweeping staircases and beautiful walled gardens three times the size of ours and laid out with statues and fountains and urns. And they were owned by these funny old widows, lame, halt, and blind, who had once been ladies and did not know how to look after themselves.

They could look after property, she said, oh, that. And

superbly. They could look after money. She would go to first one, then another in the course of a day; she had her regular days for each. She would go to Mme X and be given the money for shopping and the list. She would do the marketing and everything had to be fresh and perfect and correctly priced down to the last sou. One bad leaf on a bunch of watercress was cause for a tantrum. The shopkeepers knew she was a foreigner and tried to sell her bread that was not fresh. She would drop her proprietor's name, the shopkeeper would blench and apologize. To send one imperfect pastry to a house of that age was a disgrace.

They were full of stories, those old dames, she said, but they could not cook. What they had been trained to do was show other people how to cook. Having been raised in the house of Mary Benedicta, Mary Cicely could not boil an egg; she came away from France if not a *cordon bleu*, a dab hand at nourishing soups, beautiful portions of fish for one toothless old lady, and shopping. She said the year had proved to her that beauty comes out of pain. It must be what having a baby is like, she said.

In the last years, Philip, the routine was this: we gathered at six in the chapel. After the service, Mary Cicely and I made the breakfast. I went to school, Mary Cicely to the garden in summer, to the housekeeping closet in winter, Mary Rose to her office if she were not helping Mary Elzevir with the housework. Mary Beatrice and Mary Dorothy crept into our little parlour to sit by the fire in the winter. Somebody gave us a television set, which they turned on very low; when I came in at night I would hear Mary Dorothy mumbling the stories of soap operas to her friend. They were a source of great wonder to her.

I was allowed an hour each day to read in Mary Rose's office; I was teaching, and teaching hard. Teaching them Donne and Hopkins and Job and the Psalms. I needed this repose and took it gratefully. Then I said solitary prayers and went to the kitchen to take over so that Mary Cicely could join the others at vespers. If the meal was ready or almost ready, I set the table and joined them in the chapel.

84

I was tired; teaching always makes me tired. I had problems of my own. The school had desegregated the staff rooms. Two of the male staff had found I was an Eglantine and taken to teasing me. I tried to avoid them, but could not. This would not have bothered me had not a particularly nice man, with whom I often discussed history, taken it upon himself to defend me. I felt I was falling in love with him. I did not know where to turn.

Often, in chapel, I fancied Mary Cicely was sobbing too.

When the last summer holidays came, I found that I had become deputy sister superior by default. Mary Rose's heart was giving her trouble. Mary Dorothy was absorbed by the care of Mary Beatrice. Agnes and Cicely had their gardens. Elzevir cared only for Mary Rose.

I do not think I was as clear-headed as I ought to have been, or as charitable, for to me, the bliss of the Order was always the time it afforded me for the examination of conscience, the acquisition of tranquillity in meditation: I discovered to my horror that all my time was taken up in the labelling and ordering of trays, the dispatch of laundry bags, the addition of accounts. I had no time to read St Theresa or the Desert Fathers, whom I loved. Donne and Hopkins deserted me. Mary Agnes wanted string to tie her thyme, Mary Cicely needed a new hoe, a handle to her spade. There was another leak in the chapel roof. Mary Elzevir wanted Mary Rose's tray, and Cicely had to be called in to do it right. The television was out of order and the hydro bill was not paid. And the person to whom I was dispatching the laundry bags was now me.

But I did one or two things right: I persuaded Mary Elzevir to call a proper doctor for Sister Mary Rose, and I had a long talk with Cicely.

It was not hard to know something was wrong with her. It was simply a matter of finding her difficulty out. I stared at her, I prayed about her, I thought of talking to our confessor about her. But I could not like him. He was lean and unsympathetic. He looked at us as if we were a bunch of hens and he disliked hens. I longed to ask Mary Rose what to do, but I could not. The doctor had said that she must rest; now that I was performing with difficulty only a few of the tasks she had done for thirty years, I knew he was right; besides, Mary Elzevir would barely let me near her. I had only been let in to be given signing authority for the house, and one look at that pale face was enough. My only victory there was to insist that the doctor talk to me as well as Elzevir so that I had a record of diet and medication and the power to guard Mary Rose against Elzevir's passionate possessiveness.

Mary Rose white against the pillow. Mary Beatrice blind. Unable, even, to trace the stem of a rose in needlework; Mary Dorothy silent, in penance for her friend. Mary Agnes bent with arthritis. Mary Cicely sobbing in the dark.

I left our poor service one morning and went to her room. She was masturbating.

Oh Philip, I have seldom felt so badly. She shrieked when she saw me and hid her face in the pillows. I wanted to run away, not to find what I had found, but to hide, hide, hide. I went to back out and leave her and me in peace, or what we could disguise as peace, but she leapt up, threw her water carafe at me and cut my face above the eye, and fell down in hysterics.

Well, I had read some Freud and a lot of St Augustine in addition to his arguments against Pelagius, and our friends the Desert Fathers. I had always fancied Mary Pelagia as a Desert Father's compensatory dream. I found myself holding that poor heavy soul in my arms and letting her sob and sob; it was like piercing a dragon and watching the poison come out; and the blood from my forehead mingled with it.

She had been suffering for more than a year from the most violent sexual obsessions about our confessor, and these, of course, she felt she could not confess.

I have never felt so sorry for anyone except myself.

Mary Rose would have known the forms. I did not. I asked Cicely to come every afternoon to my room and confess herself. Sometimes I held her, because her need was violent and physical. I would even, I think, have made love to her if I had known how – do you see why I am a heretic? – but I did not feel it would help either of us, and I did not want to. I have tried to make love to women since and found that, while the spirit is willing, the flesh is simply not interested. And I think, for Mary Cicely's sake, it was just as well. Instead, I took an old line I must have heard on the farm or in English books, and had her extend her garden by three feet in each dimension, so that she was always physically exhausted.

I remember that summer with regret, almost bitterness. It was like home when Mother was sick: one resented her absence terribly.

But I was surprised by my practical ability. All my life people had been telling me I was Rita the dreamer, but you were right, Philip, when you told me I was on record as having been splendid. Rows of Macraes and Hebers, purl and plain, stood behind me as I balanced the accounts and paid the bills and did the laundry and encouraged Mary Agnes, soothed Mary Beatrice, pumped the organ.

The trouble is, however, that when I am being practical, the dreamer in me dies; I become restless and difficult and bad-tempered. It was an irritable Mary Pelagia who subscribed the whole convent to the Ontario Health Insurance Plan, a cross one who accompanied Sister Mary Rose to the Victoria Hospital and arranged that Mary Elzevir could sit there with her all day, muttering offices at appropriate hours. Sometimes I think I was even impatient with Mary Cicely, and at one time Mary Beatrice complained that I hadn't spoken to her for six days and had given her Mary Agnes's stockings, she knew them by the feel of the mends.

I confessed to the tall golden minister that I was irritable and harassed. Unctuously, he instructed me to pray for grace. Fortunately, he had failed to notice Mary Cicely's absence. I suppose we were some sort of lump to him, and he never counted us.

When, in the fall, it was time to go back to school, I felt like a pale shadow. Here was I, a mother with six children, expected to handle classrooms of teenagers all day. One night I came home and cried in Mary Cicely's lap.

"You should quit," she said.

"Mary Rose says we need the money."

"I've got money," Mary Cicely said.

I stared at her as if she was mad.

"I've got money," she said again. "I'm an orphan. I was brought up here. My mother was Sister Flora's cousin. But I've got the insurance money. It's still in a bank somewhere. Sister Mary Rose said I should never spend it."

"We must obey Sister Mary Rose."

"But if you won't lead us, who will?"

But I continued to teach and got a little better at it; I had good classes that year, I recall, and I fed them a lot of poetry. And I arranged with Sister Mary Rose that I could have an extra hour alone to myself in the evening, trying to read theology.

All my life I've hared after philosophy and theology, Philip, and, do you know, I can't tell a Pelagian from an Arminian still. I read Pascal when I want to fall asleep. I'm not only a heretic, I'm a hypocrite.

Still, the time alone helped. I suppose it was like some people's drink before dinner. It washed off the cares of one kind of life. I think now that more people should lead compartmented existences: that fewer marriages would go if there were transition rooms between job and home (other than bars), between kitchen and bedroom. Vespers after school might well have been mine, but I chose instead the solitude of the library, the soothing bindings of Sister Mary Rose's now-neglected books, and I am glad of that.

But still, but still . . . writing about one's religious life after the faith is gone is like writing about an old marriage after one has forgotten the love; acts and habits both become incredible in retrospect. Why did one struggle and suffer, what was the cause involved? I no longer remember the transparency of my attempt at the end of each teaching day to withdraw into the library and love God. I suppose I was really suing for enough spiritual quiet to remember what loving God was, else I would have been in the chapel.

But I managed, that year, I managed; although my practical side gnawed at my spirituality, I cannot say that I did not manage. I endured a painful hour with your predecessor, the other bishop, asking him, as I recall, to change our confessor. I said I did not like to tell him why, as it involved the other sisters. But I pointed out that there were things one felt one could not confess to this confessor and that I thought that for all his ability as a preacher, he was the wrong sort of person for us. The Bishop took offence. I could tell he did not intend to be put in his place by a pack of women.

"I take it you are complaining about the actions of Mr J.," he said.

"No," I said, as meekly and evenly as I could (for my managerial personality is stiff and proud, Philip), "I am complaining of the effect he has on several of our number." The several was an exaggeration, and he knew it.

"Yourself, then."

"Not myself."

"You said that there were things you did not wish to confess to him."

"I was not speaking for myself."

"You come on the advice of Sister Mary Rose?"

"Sister Mary Rose is in hospital."

"Who, then, is in charge at Eglantine House?"

This was a nasty point; I had hoped he would not see it.

"There are seven of us," I said. "Sister Mary Rose is ill. Sister Mary Elzevir has devoted herself to nursing her. Sister Mary Beatrice is blind. Sister Mary Dorothy looks after her. Sister Mary Cicely and I, temporarily, are in charge of the day-to-day operation of the house. Sister Mary Agnes, who does the cloister garden and looks after the chapel, is also failing," I added with a gulp. Sister Mary Agnes had failed so much she barely existed for us, she was a wisp that trailed from flower bed to *prie-dieu*, barely passing through what was left of our lives.

He looked down at his hands. I felt I had made a dreadful mistake. I decided to say so. "I did not come," I said, "to report on the condition of the Order, because I feel that that will change."

"How will it change?"

"If Sister Mary Rose's condition does not improve, she will make arrangements. She has said so."

"Do you know what arrangements?"

"Not precisely."

"Then your sole reason for visiting me is to ask for a more, as you say, sympathetic confessor?"

"Yes, your grace."

He frowned. He looked down at his hands, which were long and more elegant than a woman's could be. I remember thinking, he does no work, and wondering whom I could confess that to. I sat like an obedient child with my eyes cast down. He had no final authority over us unless I put us into his hands, which I was really doing. I thought in my students' language, you've goofed, Pelagia, you've done it this time, you've goofed.

Then he looked up. "You teach, do you not, Mary Pelagia?"

"Yes. At Brookford Senior High School."

"What subjects?"

"English and religious studies."

"And after school you return and manage the affairs of the Order?"

"Some of them. We live very simply. There is not much to do. The others help."

"And the Order is in need of your income?"

"Yes."

"What do you think will happen when the others go?"

"I don't know, your grace. We have no orphans. We have no novices."

"Do you worry about that?"

"The future of the Order is in the hands of Sister Mary Rose."

He held his fingertips together and pursed his lips. He looked like the Pope in a movie. "The Rev. Mr J. is leaving St Thomas's," he said.

I held my breath. I wanted to save Mary Cicely her terrible fantasies and save myself from them, too, for they were eating into my consciousness; truly, I felt, corrupting me: and I am not as unselfish as I make myself out to be.

"I would like someone young and meek," I heard myself saying. "We have all the difficulties we can bear."

"A weaker personality, then?"

"Your grace" – and oh, Philip, I am stiff-necked, it has always caused me great pain to call anyone, even the divorce judge by a title – "I have told you what the situation is. I think our need now is for gentleness."

"Is that your personal need?"

"I am the one who works in the world. The others are the ones who have been protected and will always need to be."

He thought for a moment. "I know a young divinity student. . . ."

I smiled, almost too eagerly; I had had a vision of Sister Mary Cicely romping in her garden with a young divinity student. I hoped he couldn't read me. "Whatever you choose," I said. "Whomever. Would suit."

He rose. He patted me on the head. A blessing, I suppose. "Keep me informed, Sister," he said.

I wanted to beg him not to tell Mary Rose I had come, but I knew better.

The Rev. Mr J., who had golden hair and a long nose like a proboscis, came for a week or two and then was replaced by a student deacon who was so young and limp I thought, he needs us, it will be good.

And, for a while, it was. Sister Mary Cicely at first stared at him in disbelief and wept for her lost phantom lover, but slowly either stopped suffering her sexual visions or stopped confessing them to me at night, which was a help, because in the staff room at school I was still being tortured by the two young male teachers who thought to break down my sexual reserve by

91

bringing forth all the suggestive remarks they could think of about nuns, and I was bothered, not by them, but by the colleague who defended me, one of those tall, straight-featured men I'm always attracted to: and he had entered my visions, and I was having a struggle with myself.

The shell of innocence, in fact, was broken.

When Mary Rose returned late in November, it seemed that our happiness would be resumed. Ill as she was, she superintended rituals that Mary Cicely and I had had to let fall by the wayside. But I had no more long talks with her; she was too ill for that, and besides, Mary Elzevir, gaunt in her servitude, still protected her from me like a dragon. I was jealous, but I understood, I understood.

I struggled alone with my visions. I thought of St Augustine, I thought of Pelagia, and knew my teacher friend was my sexual projection. I knew he had a wife. I knew I was the hart panting after the brook, and I knew why. My physical nature was at last asserting itself.

In my mind, I began to argue with St Augustine, with Paul, with all the Christians. If it was our nature to have these feelings, why was it evil to accept them? Why must we fight them down so hard? Surely this war she fought internally was killing Mary Cicely, who, though she seemed better, looked haggard and guilty. Surely it was better to accept that one was a physical person, suffering from a natural urge that would some day pass even if it was a distraction from God? In that sense everything was a distraction from God, the cloister garth, the garden, the embroidery in the chapel, living, even: then I understood why they had withdrawn into the desert.

It was at that point that I had what I would call my only true Eglantine vision: I saw myself standing purified and free, at the edge of a body of water, alone, dressed in white linen and holding one but one only of Margarita's pearls.

Pelagia, Marina, Margarita, Aphrodite: I was seeing myself as Venus, I think, but for a moment I thought I was a saint.

Reality – Mary Agnes's tinkling bell for vespers – called me. I left my vision grudgingly and went on to continue my fallible life.

Then a terrible thing happened. One afternoon when I was at school, Mary Cicely ran away with a young labourer she met while she was working in the garden. She might have made him a good wife, but by six o'clock the police were at the door to say that in their excitement they had run through a red light and been killed in an accident.

You know the rest. We buried her. The year dragged on. It was my turn to fall ill. The doctor advised me to take leave from school. I was delighted to return to the pseudo-idleness of convent ritual, the regimen that leaves the spirit free. I was delighted to escape the staff room and the temptation that existed for me there.

Sister Mary Rose's condition improved. She recovered enough to escape from her room and Mary Elzevir's watchful ministrations. She began to totter even to matins; I took the responsibility for raising the thermostat, which caused Mary Agnes to unbend a little. I had more time. I did more housework, without resenting it. Mary Elzevir helped me in the kitchen. I discovered she was morbidly afraid of fire.

Now we were six.

Mary Dorothy and Mary Beatrice helped when they could. Increasingly, after whichever service they had felt able to attend, they sat in front of the television set. It seemed useless to remonstrate with them.

I remember spending a good part of that winter scrubbing and polishing, trying to restore the building to the gloss that I remembered. I bought us a new vacuum cleaner and made it suck and suck the shabby, beautiful kneelers. It took the last of the pile of Miss Isbister's oriental rugs.

When our confessor came, I couldn't think of anything to confess.

Mary Rose was very weak, frail as crumbling parchment. She called me to her office. She told me she thought there was no future for me here; I was too young to remain with a dying Order. I cried and cried, but I knew she was right. My spiritual life had died – if it ever existed – in the practical details of the house. Besides, she explained, she and the others had always lived together; now there was no other young one, they would be happier to die together. It was cruelly spoken, but I knew what she meant.

I could go to the Sisters of St John in Willowdale, she said, if I felt I still had a vocation. Or I could go to a friend of hers in Toronto.

"You need someone to look after you," I said desperately. Desperate that I had not been chosen for a service I was unsuited for.

"You have done wonderful work," she said, "but you are young enough to begin again. The Sisters of St John will send us a nurse-administrator. You want your own children. You want a home, Mary Pelagia. I have been watching you. I would not feel I was right to let you stay with us."

I tried not to cry but the tears slid down my cheeks. She put out a bony hand. "I have failed you," she said, "but the flesh is weak. I must take care of Elzevir."

"You haven't failed me," I said weakly. "You couldn't have failed anyone, you are. . . ."

She cut me off and turned her head wearily, "I am, perhaps, betraying you. I think I am doing what is best. You have tried in the past to do your best. It is my turn now."

There was no use trying to discuss the matter with her. She was too ill, too tired still. I thought, I have one mother at least who knows what I ought to do.

No use to try to keep the lamps from flickering in your head.

"I will write to Maggie," she said, dismissing me.

For a while, I suffered from a nagging feeling that Sister Mary Rose wanted to be rid of me; but I knew she was an honest woman. She would have long since told me to be gone if she had felt that way. I knew that she felt I was weak in the department of the faith, but strong in perseverance. Once, you said, she mentioned to you that she had hoped I would carry on her work, but, Philip, I doubt that she was serious. After Mary Cicely was gone, I was the only one who could have; but that doesn't mean I was a serious candidate. The truth was that Mr Laidlaw died, Sister Mary Rose's heart had begun to fail, no new postulants appeared; Mary Rose knew the Order was dying and was right to push me out of it while I was still young enough to start another life.

I don't feel, as you do, that the Eglantines are a loss to the world. They were never enough of a part of it to make a difference. They served a purpose for a few good women, protected them from a world that might have hurt them, but their activities meant nothing to their society; call them a drop in the spiritual bucket and an embroidery service; that's all they were.

Goodness counts, I know. But I don't tot things up in the spiritual way any more: one more moment of serenity for God. My practical self comes astonishingly to the fore as I lead this impractical, useless life by the seashore. I am learning to see things as they are. The windhover is up there, I am here on this chair. I am not more socially useful than he is; I judge myself for it, though not severely; and I am just as willing to judge the Eglantines, bless them. It isn't given to us all to be useful, to be great.

And I know that what you are suggesting would make me more useful, but I refuse to be entangled by it.

To get back to the Eglantines: they were harmless. Dr Stern argued that they had harmed Mary Cicely, but I doubt it. Any form of Christianity and any Christian household would have been repressive for Mary Cicely at that time in history. She was pious, homely, and strongly sexed. She might have done all right staying home on the farm, met somebody at a church group . . . but the farm was gone. Mind you, Mary Rose told me she'd make several efforts to get Mary Cicely out into the world – I suppose the episode with the Mendicant Genevièves was one of them – but Cicely balked. "We had no real idea how to prepare her for the world," Mary Rose said mournfully. "We had forgotten what it was like; by implication, she decided that the world was hostile. She had the material to be what I would call a good citizen, an active wife and mother, for instance; but she prevented herself from enjoying her visits 'outside.' I blame myself very much for her fear. I ought to have pushed her. But we were so fond of her, unwilling to hurt her. I count her a great failure. I pray for her soul."

Well, Philip, I count myself a great failure, too, but I do not place this failure on the shoulders of Sister Mary Rose and the Eglantines. I suppose I never did become as much an Eglantine as Mary Cicely; my religious training militated against my becoming as absorbed in the rite and the rule as she did, since I had been brought up in a church whose religious passion was generated not by liturgy, of which we had cautious and precious little, but by hymns and fiery sermons. The structure of the Eglantines' daily lives was contained in a series of devotions which, while they hewed the line of the Book of Common Prayer and were seldom mystical and were above all cautious of Mariolatry, lifted the other sisters above mundane existence. I was fascinated by the structure and the eloquence of the texts we used, and by the gentleness, the vaporous rosiness of the atmosphere, but never quite lifted off the ground. I could understand our lives in terms of images and catch-phrases: I am the Resurrection and the Life, I saw Eternity the other night, There is no health in me . . . but my religion was, I think, aesthetic and literary only; it did not contain within it the true incense of prayer and exhortation that flows naturally and intimately from what is called the soul according to the writings of the great mystics. For me, the practical life of the Order was the only salvation, and that robbed me of its sacramentalism, so I had to leave.

So much romanticism about nuns: from the black romance where non-sex generates frenzied sexual fantasy, to what I called the romance of renunciation and, more recently, the romance of the failure of renunciation. And what were we, really, but a kind of ashram. We began to fall apart when our guru had a heart attack. Who protected us from history.

So I wound up as Maggie Hibbert's *au pair* girl, Maggie being a clever woman who, in exchange for domestic work, gave lessons in Society. A lot of people thought she was Catholic, she has so many children. Sister Mary Rose thought her an excellent woman. The change in my life was sudden and violent.

*   *   *

I remember only vaguely how I got to Maggie Hibbert's house. In the back, I think, of a black car. Who sat in front I do not know. In the back with me sat Loss, round, complete, an enormous egg. I clung to it and wept.

What had I lost that I did not have to lose? Family? Innocence? I did not know then. But my loss was an egg and it had one of those faces on it Mother used to draw on our eggs when she was in good humour: a face with a terrible frown; and I could not reverse it, turn it upright, to a smile. It was too big for me, my arms could not encompass it.

Loss, big egg, big O, big nothing. Big nothing and I on our way to Toronto.

Not knowing that out of big nothing, little nothing grows.

Rationally, I knew why I was going to Maggie's; I knew a little of why I felt so badly, even. Sister Mary Rose had had to choose between me and the others. In the little life that was left to her, she had chosen to give her care to her coevals, which was surely just. Mary Elzevir's terribly possessiveness had grown around Mary Rose like a hedge of thorns, it had openings for the other two she had known a long time, but not for me. It was only Christian of me to retreat, leave them all in peace. I understood that. But that afternoon in the car I felt what I was giving up, felt it in a way that I had not been able to feel it for years; not the fact of Eglantine House, but the ideal: that a community could improve the world. And the feeling that now I could only improve the community by leaving it was a bitter one.

Mary Rose and I had talked it out as well as Elzevir had permitted it; and when I was in Mary Rose's presence, I understood what she said. There was always a kind of sanity in her office that did not pertain for me elsewhere.

But there is no arguing that once I left her room I felt cast out, and the journey to Maggie's was a fearful one, through time (from Mediaeval to Modern, as our old history text used to be called) and through space: the space between provincial London and sophisticated Toronto is still very wide.

97

So that as I drew closer to Toronto, farther from the powerfully kind orbit of Sister Mary Rose, I saw myself less and less as someone misplaced among dying women, and more and more as an exile, a sacrifice to the number stamped on the arm of Mary Elzevir, who became a Christian not to reject her people, but to pray for her dead.

But I also had my dead. My father had died during my second year in the convent. Mother had not invited me home for the funeral. I had to mourn him after the fact. I wrote her as many comforting letters as I could, knowing she would be grieving badly even if she never showed a tear. I went to see her once or twice, but she did not unbend to me. She kept herself tight and erect, as separate from me as if I were a visiting stranger. To be treated so formally in my own house made me weep.

"You don't need to come back," she said. "They're your family now. And I'm all right. I manage. The neighbours are good to me. Stuart came home a month ago and I said, 'If you've left me this long, you can leave me for good.' You can't play fast and loose with people, Rita."

As always, her face was full of hurt pride. I looked at her and wondered who had hurt her, for I knew now that it was not I, nor Stuart, nor Shirley, nor my father either. Somewhere, buried in her past, was a lash she could not forget, that she expected again, and again and again. That she invented. That she could not live without. If all of us had prospered on exactly her terms, been ministers, kindergarten teachers, whatever she wanted, we would never have pleased her. What her heart demanded was failure, she had sung Newman's hymn too often, all she wanted was for change to be decay. I looked at her and pitied her. I never saw her again.

When she died four years later, I was again deprived of ceremony. Shirl came up from Texas but did not find my address until after Mother was buried. I got home in time to help her empty the house and close it up. We had two good days together, going through the meagre family possessions, remarking on all the deaths and vanishings. Mother had died alone and my heart felt wind-blasted for her, but I knew she had wanted to end that way, alone and afraid. Shirl did not agree. "She loved us all when we could get through to her," she said. "When Ernie and I were divorced she said she'd never speak to me again and I kept bringing the kids here, I just made her. I brought her down to Texas once – you should come and see us, you'd like Jack, and I know they don't keep you tied up in ropes at your house – and she had a real good time. You don't understand her. You're too much like her in a way, Rita: proud."

Peacock bought the land. I had him store some of our furniture in the barn for us, too. Was I thinking already of leaving the convent? I don't think so. I simply knew that good maple dressers were hard to find and Shirley's kids might like them, no matter how funny and un-Texan she thought they were.

I had a good time with our Shirley, ever-cheerful, ever-accepting. She said Mother had died in a tidy house. Aunt Jean had taken to checking on her every day and found her dead at the end. She didn't appear to have suffered much. I remembered the way she put her hand on her heart when she was angry; I had thought it an affectation.

It was good to be back on the line for a while. I even went up to see Eddie, but he was out, and I felt lucky. Mary and Doog were long gone but Bill and Jean had survived, and Aunt Hilda in Sarnia. I could tell they thought me odd, but I had that warm feeling of being with my family, as if I were an old dog by the fire.

When Shirley went back to her family and I had to stay on alone to close the sale, the emptiness slapped me: big nothing again. A void I had met before, before I was born even, and would meet again. I was never able to fill that void with prayer, Philip. It was born in me.

The tulips on the wallpaper ticked like clocks. The linoleum squeaked under my knees as I tried to pray. I wandered the empty house, finding my parents' meagre existences (How they would hate me to call them that, though! It shows how I still fail to understand) recorded not in a family Bible but on little scraps of paper, backs of envelopes: *2/6/42 Rosie pigged; 8/7/47, McCrory, $18; bread, milk, soda biscuits, Certo; Mr B. re Rita's report.* . . .

There was no Bible. Only a dictionary, an automotive hand-book, a collection of old school texts. My mother must have taken to reading them late in her life; a lot of the poems were underlined and annotated in her schoolgirl's hand.

Stu came up from Detroit to help deal with the lawyers. He objected to everything we'd done, got drunk, kicked a hole in the kitchen wall, called me every obscenity. I had at least the sense not to promise to pray for him.

Loss: After the funeral was paid for we each had a thousand dollars apiece from the sale of the property. I'd have divided my share between Stu and Shirl, but I didn't want him to take it and drink it, so I paid for the tombstone Mother had ordered, that had never been put up. And saw it in place. That was, I thought, the end of West China for me.

Loss: the 401 Macdonald-Cartier (why do I always think Mackenzie-Papineau?) highway cuts through bush straight from London to Toronto. Big green signs and arrows and pro-liferations of symbols no one but civil servants can understand; I had somehow expected to take the old Dundas Street way, it was so long since I had been to Toronto; but they sped me ef-ficently beside my egg through fields and airports and suburbs and trees.

Loss: I was empty. I incorporated my egg. I was a white, swollen thing, gut-blown before painting.

I see men as trees walking. . . .

They had to help me into Maggie's house. It had black and white tiles on the floor in the hall. It smelled funny. It smelled: male.

Here, the air smells of iodine and flowers. There is the regular irregularity of the tide, the shallow estuaries' rhythm as they fill and empty themselves. The birds are bold. The weather changes at noon. I can put all my loss, all my forgetting, on this landscape; spread my wrack on the sandbars and let the sea carry it away.

*   *   *

I was led into Maggie's house like a shame-faced schoolgirl. I remember, first, the black and white tiles; then the smell; then Maggie's eyes, dark, close-together, sharp.

I won't say much more about her; she was good to me, and she was your friend. You came in late, once, Bishop of Huron, Philip Yurn, and I was a guest then, not the help, ready to sit beside you because someone more secular might have been afraid, and you kissed Maggie in that way city people have of making a half-embrace a greeting, and gave Phoebe your coat and – I loved you at once for it – clipped your white sheepskin earmuffs around her banister. There! Ready. Rubbed your cold hands and received your single-malt and smiled.

I was not born to like Maggie; neither of us took naturally to the other; we were not, as my mother used to say, the same breed of cat. But she was good to me, always has been; small, short-bodied, immensely practical, as one has to be to manage a husband and five boys and a house and a girl. And she had taken a good many of us in: those were the years of the emptying of the cloisters. You could say she used us, if you wanted to be hard, but in fact she gave a great deal more than she got. And one doesn't have to have a natural affinity for a person to value her. She had a list and a method for handling every situation; she had been brought up that way; she ordered her world and that of those around her with labels and lists. If it seemed odd at the time to go from Eglantine order to Maggie order, it was good. I should never have survived freedom.

The first days in that house are lost in the swilling mists of the smell of socks. In a bewilderment, a cringing feeling of inferiority to Maggie, to her world. An unwillingness to deal with it. Whenever I had a moment off I would creep up to her attic and crawl, even in the late summer heat, under my eiderdown. Maggie could sense in a second my departures. I would hear her on the stairs and she would uncover me like greased lightning. "That's not allowed," she would say. "Up and on your feet. Come and help me pack the things for the cottage."

The boys, or some of them, were away, I recall. At camp. In the bush. At their friends'. But the house never seemed to recover from the pervasive smell of their socks; it was apparent to me only, who had spent so many years away from such a scent.

We had a few days alone, then; black-eyed Maggie, gentle Tom, a tall, thin, pale man, personality wiped away by the strength of his family's, a pastel among acrylic targets. Maggie explained their life to me as if I were a kindergartener. Which I was.

I liked little Phoebe; she was small, and pale like her father. The others were simply overpowering.

The house was, as well. It was big, almost as big as Eglantine House, remember? And beautifully decorated: big paintings, thick rugs, magnificent old furniture from both their families. Maggie had the female passion for flowers and had them everywhere. None of the spider plants you find dangling in windows now: masses of whatever was in season. Tom made good money at the law firm, and Maggie had some of her own.

I had some money, too; in fact, a good deal. Mary Rose had returned to me a large proportion of what I had brought in to Eglantine House, over my protests. She said I would need it. I did, more than I had imagined, for Maggie kept hauling me off to the stores. That first fortnight I spent awkward lengths of time in fitting rooms, standing in front of mirrors trying on, before Maggie's all-seeing eyes, garments more and more garish. "You're through with navy blue!" she would say half maliciously. "Try this, and this, and this. . . ."

Poor Maggie, she went to a great deal of trouble over me and I feel I ought to have been more of a success. First, there was the matter of clothing. We stood in fitting rooms, while the fluorescent lights greyed and sallowed my skin, trying on everything in every department store. It was the year of the mini-dress, which did not help. Maggie had banned navy blue and was determined to make me look smart, but, having gone to high school when it was fashionable to wear one's skirts to one's bobby socks, I was horrified by the idea of showing my legs, which were never a fine point. Maggie was going to insist until, standing foolish in a curtailed brown dotted-swiss frock with a yoke and puffed sleeves, I turned to her and committed my first piece of worldly wit: "Have you got my hairbow?" In Baby Snooks' voice. We collapsed. We got on better than I remembered.

When I think of it, I hadn't even worn a brassiere for years; it took me ages to think of jeans as not being rude. I put dresses on for her and stood awkward in front of mirrors like a sulky teenager, and she comforted me.

When the boys came back, I felt better. There was always an endless amount to do. We were in a constant panic over food. The boys ran from Bellman, who was twenty-two and at university, down to Little Chris, who was six foot four at the age of fifteen. No wonder Phoebe always looked crushed.

During that first month Maggie was like a tonic thrust down my throat. Without her, I could never have faced even a fragment of the world. She rushed me from store to store, had my hair cut, chose my underclothes, chose my shoes. I was helpless as a baby and she knew it.

Sometimes at night I cried and cried, not from weariness but from homesickness. Maggie would come up to me. She was gentle. I saw the mother in her. She asked if I had any family. I told her how Father had died and Mother had not asked me home to the funeral; how Mother died, how we sold to Peacock. About Stu in Detroit, drinking. Shirley in Texas, lost, though: mail always came back from her old address. John, but I did not know where John was. Her face clouded when I mentioned Christabel Clavering but she said nothing. Then, "You really are alone, aren't you? You'll have to make a real effort, then. Pull yourself together, make friends. That's what you came out for, isn't it?"

I shook my head, a miserable child. "They're all dying," I sobbed. "They asked me to go so they could die in peace."

She thought a moment. "That's harder. Look, I'm going to

need you this fall. I'm starting law school, but as soon as we get a routine going I'll ask if they need you to teach at St Mildred's or St Clement's or some place, huh? I don't want you to go broody on me."

She seemed to be softer after that, and once everyone was home, it was hard to brood in that house. There was eternal washing to do, eternal potato-peeling, eternal shopping. Phoebe, who seemed a lonesome child, to talk to. And there were always two dinners at night, one for the mob, one for the adults and their guests.

There were a lot of guests. Tom had a large practice and was also involved in some way in Liberal politics. Maggie had friends from her activities in the church; she also, for some reason, knew a lot of artists – that was her excuse for putting me on the Pill, she sweet-talked me by saying you never could tell what would happen with her artists – and people from what she called "all walks of life," though none, I ever felt, from mine, whatever it was.

I liked the domestic routine. For some reason I don't resent housework; I can think of other things while I do it; it releases my mind. And the boys were fun, elephantine, joshing things, horny bastards one minute and big kids the next. When we all sat in church together I took great joy in the scrub-knuckled row of them: they were like country boys.

Rock music and dirty feet, mounds of mashed potatoes, knees to patch, bundles of dirty sheets: it was like being on the farm again. Phoebe sitting on the counter asking me all about the Eglantines and could we start a garden like theirs in the spring.

It was the parties I didn't like. The dresses Maggie had picked out for me were strappy and naked. I felt an awful fool in them, as if I were going about in night dresses. I passed out cocktails when I could, though she hired a bartender whenever there were more than a dozen guests, which was often. She put great wasteful spreads of fruit and meat and cheese on the dining-room table to, as she said, soak up the alcohol, and almost forbiddingly introduced me to the mob. Woe to me if she caught me in the kitchen fetching ice for Albert the barkeep. "He knows where it is and you don't know anyone," she would say grimly.

I felt like a fool and a wastrel, but I met a few people I liked. I had a certain coinage as well; in that decade the ex-nun was desirable in the sense that the deaf and dumb nymphomaniac whose father owned a brewery had been in mine. Soon enough I was trying to escape dinner engagements by saying I had to babysit Phoebe, and Maggie was shouting that Chris or Bitsy or Boo was going to be home, go on out. I had to let wife-hunting lawyers spend money on me. It was very immoral, I felt.

And I was immoral, too. You can tell from my description, Philip, that I had left the convent physically as well as mentally; the chemistry of the house was beginning to work on me. The big boys, untying my apron strings with thick, clumsy fingers, pinching my bottom as I leaned to get things out of the oven, began to be a torment to me. I began to have great, guilty longings for the second-eldest, Matt, who somehow took the curse off the memory of the country boys who had fumbled for me, and opened a whole new world. He made me feel, obscurely, that there was some sort of future, something to live for. I could say crudely – I will – that he got my hormones working with his grunts and his comic embraces as I rushed around the house.

I suppose that's what sex is for, isn't it? It increases the will to live. Perhaps our lives should end (our natural lives, not our convent, cubicle, scholarly lives) when our sex urge dies.

At any rate, I wish I had listened harder to what my body was telling me, instead of being so darn relieved when he went off to Queen's.

Then the dreadful news about John and Christabel came.

As a couple, they had made out predictably badly. They began with little money and continued with little, though Christabel's father, when they moved to Toronto, had bought them a house in a distant suburb. She had had three babies in a row and had no idea how to manage them. I believe her old nannie came to help for a while, but neither she nor John had any idea of how to look after themselves or handle what money he did bring home. She had a curious idea as well that children's clothing could be bought only from Holt-Renfrew, and another that children bring themselves up. I had heard first from my mother, then from Uncle Stanley, that they were getting on less than well. John needed quiet for his work, stayed away more and more; annoyed his department chairman by being egg-spotted and odd-socked; expected Christabel to manage as Hebers always do, with efficiency on nothing and on principle. Calamity led to calamity. She drank, had affairs, failed to notice outbreaks of eczema and impetigo, put on weight, let her teeth go. One night, when John was at the Learned Societies' meeting somewhere out west, she managed to let the house in Wishing Well Acres burn to the ground. The oldest child, sleeping over at a friend's, was saved. Christabel, surveying the ruins, screeched, leaped into a neighbour's car, and drove away from the scene.

Uncle Stanley put me in touch with John; Aunt Frieda was dying and he couldn't manage. I got Maggie's minister to do the children's funeral, found John and young Michael a place near the university, dealt with the inquests and the insurance money, and spent long evenings with John letting him talk and drink to a whimper. To my amazement Colonel Clavering came several times to see his grandson and talk to John. He was not of a class of person who believes in intimacy, but he was kinder than I had in my reverse-snobbish heart expected him to be.

The police found the neighbour's car, but never Christabel.

Maggie invited John to several of her parties that winter, but he hung like a ghost in corners, muttering about Michael. Eventually we brought Michael to the house for a while while John pulled himself together. He was quite a good philosopher, John, though very bad at matching socks. No one could help him much. Uncle Stanley gave him an old ulster to replace his winter coat, and he wrapped himself in that and began a slow recovery. Michael thrived in Maggie's house, with Phoebe to talk to and the big boys to look up to. It was always a shock to look at him and see Christabel's high white forehead, Christabel's flower eyes.

Meanwhile, I was adjusting myself to the fact that in the great world it is not evil to dress well or lead a social life. I was awkward, but, once I grasped this simple fact of adult existence, more comfortable. I began to pick and choose among Maggie's young men (so did she, I think, but that's telling) and find some of them good. There was a class that was patently wife-hunting, which took you out for a drink and quizzed you like a detective in a British novel. If you liked the same movies, symphonies, books, and food, you passed. I learned to avoid young men of twenty-seven serious about the future. I preferred young monomaniacs who would take you out and talk all evening about bird-watching or François Truffaut.

Just before Christmas, Maggie had a very large party. She combined the Political List, the Law List, and the Artists' List, and the house was jammed. Everywhere, she and Phoebe and Michael had hung mistletoe. Albert the bartender had brought two assistants, food was laid out on all surfaces in addition to the diningroom table, I defied Maggie by buying an evening dress that was navy blue, but shiny and very sexy, so she forgave me, the boys invited their own friends so the house rocked with their music upstairs, the rooms were smokey and full of laughter and jammed.

I found myself pushed into a corner against a tall man, giggled, looked up. It was Asher Bowen. He was still beautiful, but very bald. And he didn't ask me to dinner, he asked me to church.

"Ash Bone, Ash Bone," I hear Stuart's mournful cry. But then the bell tolled differently; I saw his parents' house, a Palladian ghost on the riverbank behind a screen of birches and daffodils. Ash trees on the shore turned glorious gold-orange in the fall. The boy glimpsed from the locker room. Home, but with a curious exaltation, again.

He was a lawyer now. No, he had not taken over his father's firm in the provinces, he practised in Toronto. Same building as Tom Hibbert. One of those firms with six or seven mellifluous names and one Slavic just to keep up with the times. No, he didn't go back much; his parents were dead, he hadn't been back since he had their furniture stored and sold the house. It wasn't as big as it looked from the road; in fact when he went back it looked very small and shabby; his father had fallen out with the world; ended his days there alone. An oil company had bought the property: there was no fighting history. The refineries were moving down river, and that was that.

It was what is called a whirlwind romance. We spun into each other's arms. He was beautiful, he was from home, he wanted *me*. And he said his prayers. I don't like to think now what I was to him. I mentioned Mr Laidlaw and Heberville, but I never quite got to telling him about the gas station.

Both our parents were dead. We were past the normal age for marrying. We were free agents, free to choose each other. We had collided. We decided it was meant.

It is hard to remember being in love; there are those who have called it an illness; they are probably right. It's a kind of obsession, a glorious one when it works. And Asher, besides the brilliance of his looks, had a kind of intensity that I envied, coveted almost. When I sat beside him in church I felt that his words flew up to God far faster than mine; they must, he was fiercely concentrated, as single as Mary Elzevir in her raptures in chapel, his knuckles whitened when he prayed.

Two years later, I met you. I was the chatelaine of an enormous house in lower Forest Hill, filled with his parents' excellent antiques. My belly was round and you congratulated me. Then you looked at Ash over Maggie's peonies. "And how," you asked, "does your husband enjoy being married to one who was once the bride of Christ?"

I looked over at Asher. He had the look of a hawk about to pounce on a tremulous vole. I turned back to you and babbled about the Eglantines. You became my friend, my consolation. After all, Asher could not object to bishops coming to call as he had to Michael and to John.

I asked Dr Stern, years later, how long in his experience it took people to realize they had married the wrong persons; he said, "Two years," in a cracked kind of voice that led me to wonder if it had happened to him, too. But he never told.

As I said, it was a whirlwind romance. I invested Asher with all my emptiness, I made him God, home, Mary Rose, family. It is as hard to remember the intensity of that period as it is to remember the reasons I joined the Eglantines, the non-rational ones at least, but my spring with him was a magic spring, and as the trees were coming out we were married. He bought a beautiful big old house for us and furnished it with his mother's beautiful things, even hired a gardener to look after the grounds and a housekeeper because the place was too big for me. I felt like a queen.

He filled my emptiness, though later I was to complain he had taken me over. He told me what to wear and in a week I was as camel-hair conservative as my blue-haired neighbours. He decided that I should go back to school and I was soon beginning an M.A. in philosophy; I would rather have started a baby, but, as he said, it was early days yet. I loved to set the table at night with his mother's soft old silver. We always had flowers. It might be profitable to be a florist in Toronto.

I was empty; I handed my void to him. He told me what to wear, what to do; when he knew me better, he often told me what I felt. He filled my mind, my thoughts, my body. He sat beside me in church. During sacraments his face gleamed pale and fanatic; he had an intensity I had never seen in any Eglantine but Mary Elzevir. I loved him very much indeed.

I would wake in the morning beside him and think what a miracle my life was. Timidly stroking his back and shoulders. Not so he could feel me. Just to reassure myself that my miracle, my beautiful, rigid knight was still there. Sometimes I lay and stared at the ceiling and thought how different my life was from Mother's, pumping gas and gathering eggs. I never liked hens.

Let's go back; I'm going too fast, rushing headlong down the halls of my story to avoid something. Let me listen to the paper boats in the underground streams.

I'm at Maggie's. I have come from Eglantine House. At Maggie's, I behave like an obedient child. I dress as she tells me to, hand the cocktails round. At Maggie's a great many people are looking for partners, and for the first time my sexuality is allowed to come out. Her four big sons chase me round the kitchen to keep me in practice and even her quiet husband has not indicated that I am unappetizing.

Socially, I have no world of my own, but this does not matter, for when Maggie entertains, the guests are not labelled. They seem to like me. Some of them are writers and artists, some are politicians, some come from Tom's legal world.

They are not rich, but they are well off, Maggie and Tom. They have old furniture and silver: good and plain. They do not dress as well as their guests, and they are not cynics; they are openly Christian. Sometimes I find Maggie's Christianity on the muscular side, but it makes her house more comfortable for me. Someone I'd seen on television once turned to me and said, once, "Always a lot of church boffins here, aren't there? Raoul calls this place the Clergy Reserve." I didn't mind.

Maggie's friends are very married, very marrying. She has married off a great many nuns, she says. The Episcopalians send her sisters from upstate New York and Chicago and she's had an Ursuline or two. She loves a wedding. Often her friends are back-achingly pregnant among her potted plants. Often, too, her friends are potted. It's rather like Christabel's cottage sometimes. But I feel more at home here, much more at home.

I stand among Maggie's friends, offering drinks, seeing Phoebe does not get out of hand or the boys shoot a Frisbee down the front stairs. I answer the door. The beautiful people come in (it is the age of the beautiful people, just before the swingers) and their eyes roll back as they look for friends or the super-beautiful people, journalists, Tom's legal cronies, famous politicians. Christabel, I think, Christabel would have liked it here.

Dinner parties are small and often quiet. The evening cocktail parties are the big ones. Maggie covers the round table with food and hires a maid to bring hot *hors d'oeuvres*, and

Albert the barman to dispense huge measures of rye and scotch and gin in frosty glasses. I run a lot, refilling the ice jug from bags in the pantry. Sometimes the boys and I run to the neighbourhood ice machine. At ten, I put Phoebe to bed. It is no use going myself, for my bedroom is over the diningroom and the noise is unbelievable. I go downstairs again. The beautiful people are all very involved in each other. I talk to the pregnant wives: I wish I were one of them.

Then Asher walks in.

Oh dear, it really was a very foolish marriage.

"You know," he says, "I think I've seen you before."

"You have," I say. "We were at the same high school together." (Careful not to call it the Kleeget.) "West China."

"Oh yes. I took my grade thirteen there. My mother was ill."

"I was in grade nine. Your father was the judge."

"Were you from the town?"

"Down the river. Heberville."

"Not too far from us."

"We used to pass your place on the bus. There were daffodils in the woods."

"My mother was English."

"Do you ever go back there now?"

"No. They've both passed away. All I have of them is their furniture in storage. I'd get it out if I had a wife. Do you go home?"

"There's no one I know left except an old uncle I can't stand. The good really do die young."

"Where do you live? I'll take you home out of all this racket if you like."

"I live here."

"Are you one of Maggie's nuns? You weren't an Eglantine by any chance?"

"Do you know about them? Not many people do."

"I did Greek with an old gent who used to talk about them very fondly."

I discovered that I longed to talk to Ash Bowen about the Eglantines. I put Phoebe to bed and went with him to mid-

111

night Mass. Before the evening was out he had christened me Peggy. Rita reminded him of a song he didn't like, and I had never got used to Marguerite. And of course Pelagia wouldn't do.

We also settled on a church to go to together.

Poor Pelagia, she is supposed to be in heaven now, but I somehow always imagine her under the sea. Knitting sweaters for drowned sailors. Among the mer-people.

We were married very quickly. I was surrounded by Hibberts, Maggie's enormous gang. I wore a pink suit, I think, and Phoebe was dressed up in a white dress and had flowers. Asher's best friend, Jim Tally, stood up with him, and his secretary, Amabel Webster, was there, too, and Michael and John.

We went on a proper honeymoon to Bermuda; made love, rode bicycles and swam. I felt I was in heaven with Pelagia, then.

Asher loved order, routine. An object out of place disturbed him. If, instead, in the fall, of sticking to my Husserl and my Heidegger, I absently moved one of his mother's beautiful Chinese blue and white pots an inch out of line, he would frown and replace it. In fact, he made a nightly round of the house, just to see if everything was in place.

I did the cooking. He had to be careful of his stomach. The food was very plain. The delicious French things Cicely had taught me to make were simplified, then eliminated. Everything had to be very delicately seasoned and, mostly, steamed. I thought he would have liked that restaurant Grandma Heber took us to as children, the Diet Kitchen.

He liked to watch me work in the kitchen. He said I reminded him of their cook at home, old Effie Macrae. My heart dropped like a stone. I never did get around to telling him about the French Line. I excused myself on the grounds that it sounded worse than it was, but I knew it was because neither he nor I accepted the legend that Hebers were as good as anyone in the world; and though I felt obscurely inferior to him, as I did to many people, I didn't feel particularly inferior in any one way; I deferred to his taste, his worldly experience, as a good wife should. But I did not then feel as if we were King Cophetua and the Beggar Maid.

Ash was, on the whole, a silent man. He told me little about himself beyond his experiences with Mr Laidlaw and how he hated the year he had spent at the collegiate. I would find things out about him from his friends – how he'd fallen in love once and almost failed second year law, for instance, how he'd been considered, as a child, frail – this from John, who knew more about the Bowens than I did, though he didn't say much, for Asher had no love for John's slouching presence in Stanley's ulster. He called him my crazy cousin. I used to meet John at the university when I wanted to see him.

If Ash wasn't fond of John, I did not warm to Jim Tally, who seemed to come to dinner every other night. I suppose I was jealous of his intimacy with Asher, for after dinner they always retired to Asher's office with coffee and brandy and left me alone with my philosophers. Tally wasn't a lawyer – I've never found out what he did, he sounded like a gossip columnist to me – but he was very close to Asher. He had a way of hunching up his shoulders and looking very Irish (which he was) and conspiratorial.

We led a very quiet life. I went to school, read my philosophy, which was dry, wrote infantile papers. I found it very difficult to remember philosophy and still do; Asher said he thought this was just as well, I could read the same books over and over, what a saving. So I read them over and over, retaining just enough to pass my examinations, then forgetting. Sometimes I still wake up in the middle of the night worrying about Occam's Razor. (Is it really 'Less is More' and if it is that, what does that mean? Where's my book?) I wasn't unhappy, but I didn't, either, feel that I was leading quite the life I had expected as a married woman. I wanted a child.

Asher thought we had better put it off for a bit, but I was worried. I was well over thirty. Towards the end of our second year I did, in the end, become pregnant. Asher looked at me; "You won't let it interfere with your studies, will you?" I pointed out all the women in graduate school who carried babes on their back and gave him a copy of *The Millstone*.

I was a bit of a cheat, wasn't I?

Maggie kept in touch; dropped in a lot. Once she asked me if I couldn't get Asher to come back to St Simon and St Jude with them but I told her he was devoted to St Mary Magdalene, sung Eucharist, genuflecting, he thought St Simon too low.

"And you?" she asked.

I said I didn't mind. Wherever he wanted to go was fine with me.

"Is it like the convent, St Mary Mag?"

"Oh no. Sister Mary Rose couldn't carry a tune. We weren't allowed communion more than once a week."

"He's a funny man," Maggie said. Fishing, I thought. I said nothing. "I bet he says his prayers before he gets into bed."

"Of course."

"Tom used to do it until I asked him if he was getting up the courage or purifying the act."

There wasn't anything to say to that either so I changed the subject, I don't remember to what. But there were things I knew I wasn't going to tell Maggie or anyone else. She'd have loved a tour of the house, but I wasn't going to take her upstairs and let her tell it all over town that we now had separate rooms.

That had come about in a way I now find strange and significant. Asher had bought the house alone and had had it decorated without consulting me, as a surprise. It was beautifully done, but the master bedroom was black and brown and white with brass-bound mahogany furniture: a room for a bachelor or a monk. He had a surprising number of suits, and there was hardly room for my skimpy wardrobe in the closet, an excuse I later made use of. I had to, because the final coup de théâtre was, over the bed, a large, very green, very naked, Spanish primitive painting of the crucifixion.

I was, on the whole, very passive with Asher. I thought he knew best and I knew nothing, which was more or less true.

But about six months after we came home from Bermuda, I put my foot down about the painting. I did not like being made love to under the dead eyes of a hysterically Jesuitical, unresurrectible Jesus, and I said so.

Asher was very angry. He had picked it up in Spain, he said, it was very good, and it represented an important period in his life to him – he had actually made a pilgrimage to Santiago de Compostela – and he made me a little homily on wifely obedience and Christian marriage. This did not impress me, and I was surprised to hear that he took the "obey" in the marriage service so seriously. I stated simply that in a house with five bedrooms, four unoccupied, there was no need to screw under an obviously sex-hating icon. I was surprised by my fervour and Asher was surprised by my language. The lawyers made a great point of it later. They said that every time he wanted sex he had to overcome his loathing for pink chenille. All my lawyer said was "There are worse things."

But I didn't tell Maggie. I still had a little dignity left and I wanted Asher to have some as well. It would have made too funny a story at a party. I just said, "What this house needs is babies."

"I can't see Ash with a babe on his knee, can you?"

"I can't see me," I said. In fact, I was very involved with being the Sistine Madonna and the only place Ash fitted in was as an El Greco St Joseph so I'd thrown him out of the picture.

"Put a gate across the livingroom door," said Maggie. "Get a washer and dryer and dishwasher. You're letting him live like a bachelor, sending the sheets out and keeping Mrs Macpherson. Don't let him foist a nannie on you, you've got too much help already. Put the kid down for the YMHA nursery school right away, it's got a waiting list like Eton." She looked at me and I wasn't paying attention. "Do you even know what babies are like, Rita? They're sticky. Can you see Asher all sticky? You're going to have to watch it, or you'll get in a mess with that kid. If I were you I'd give all those goddamn Chinese pots to the museum and put a few nicks in the furniture right now."

I decided she was a destructive influence and went back to being the Sistine Madonna.

*   *   *

I had hoped to do natural childbirth with Asher holding my hand and counting, but the Ashers of this world are not meant for such experiences, and neither, it turned out, was I. After a long and difficult labour I held out my arms for my apotheosis, my child. It was not given to me. I fell asleep. I woke hearing Asher saying:

> Thou shalt not kill
> But needst not strive
> Officiously
> To keep alive.

I began to scream.

Asher called him Charles and I called him Chummy, and he was hydrocephalic. Fortunately, he was otherwise normal. There was no trouble with malformed innards, for instance, no genuine malformation of the brain. He looked almost normal, although he was very delicate. He wasn't, I pointed out to Asher, a monster. After the first operation, which involved inserting a shunt to drain off the excess fluid, we thought he would be fine. I set out to be the best mum of a hydrocephalic child that ever was, unaware that Asher was bleeding to death inside.

Chummy stayed in the hospital for four months after he was born, but I went to see him and hold him every day, so he would know me. I joined societies for the parents of defective children, I learned what I could about his condition, I did everything but register at medical school. Ash had suggested once that we consign him to a children's home, but both the neurologist and I were appalled: he was going to be all right. He might not, the doctor said, live past the age of ten, but he might, on the other hand, given the technical facilities now available, reach maturity and beyond with a normal intelligence.

Asher had left to me the job of studying the clinical charts, learning how to handle Chummy. He said it was a specialist's job and with all these neurologists' bills (though most of them were covered by insurance) he would have to work longer hours. I was content with my new obsession. Chummy was more interesting than Heidegger. The problems were keeping him disease-free and making sure he progressed through the ordinary stages of infancy, some of which had been by-passed in hospital. I divided my time between being a nurse and a physiotherapist.

I enjoyed it, mind you. You remember Chummy. When he was well, he was a lovely, affectionate child. When he was ill, he was always a challenge, and I love a challenge. I came to be one of the worst amateur neurologists in Toronto.

But it was not easy. He was tantrumous and given, when his shunt had gone wrong, to violent rages. He was, like all babies, untidy. Asher's immaculate house began to show signs of wear and tear. Mrs Macpherson left in disgust. She said she didn't like the look of the babe, he had the evil eye. I had not thought that that concept had reached as far north as Scotland and took umbrage. She was replaced by a series of women who were even more superstitious about him, or disliked me. I am not very good, to tell the truth, at imposing routines on other people, though I like to live by them myself.

If I remember anything at all about that period, it was that we lived an empty life. I was almost totally preoccupied with Chummy, Asher with his practice. We couldn't use ordinary babysitters, so unless Phoebe was free or we had a live-in nurse, we went out very little. We even went to church separately most of the time – I to Maggie's St Simon's because it was closer, Asher to St Mary Mag's with its incense and ghosts – because we couldn't take Chummy with us. Because it was impossible to correct him firmly, he was, after the age of two, considerably spoiled. He learned to fake seizures when he was crossed, the little beggar, like a Siamese cat.

I can't say that Asher and I grew apart. I think we were always apart. I cannot now imagine two people less likely to become, in time, Baucis and Philemon. We were not chips off the same block, limbs from the same tree. All we had in common, at bottom, was the church and Mr Laidlaw. Mr Laidlaw was dead, we went to different churches now, and a vision from a locker room door, I was finding, was not sustaining.

We were so different, Ash and I; in a way, he was life-denying, with his black and brass furniture and grey-green Christ. He was restrained, refined, autocratic, and eloquent in court (very rarely I went to hear him plead a case and he looked wonderful in his gown and tab-collar, like a curate on the way up). I was none of those things, and I had begun to put on weight, a cardinal sin in Canadian womanhood, though I argued that it was natural, all my family did it, then got rake thin after the reproductive period was over. (Ash's reply to this was, "On that basis you could argue that adultery was normal too." It made me wish he'd been strangled at birth.)

He was a snob, Ash. A spoiled brat. I'm still angry at him. Angry at myself for mistakenly marrying him. My heart is not clear. I can't do what you ask, Philip.

Well, you knew us at that time. You, and Maggie and Tom, a few others. I also saw John and Michael the odd time, and visited Uncle Stanley, who was dying. He'd never thought much of my religious ideas; he was an atheist as most Marxists are, but whenever I was in the neighbourhood I dropped in just to get one of those wiry country-uncle hugs and prove that I had a family and it was good.

Who else did we see? What did we do? There was the time when Asher got sick and his doctor thought he had multiple sclerosis, and he took to his bed. After the first weeks of serious illness were over, it turned into rather a good time, for he was home with us, and he would sit up, pale as his crucifixion, against his pillows and read to Chummy beside him, pick at his tray, ask me to run errands for him. He was sweet and rather needy, not querulous at all.

For a while, he worked at home. I got him books from his office and medical books from the library (he was keen on his symptoms and read about them a lot and grew new ones), and then, and this pleased me very much, Amabel, his secretary, a fat, gutsy woman, took to coming every day to take dictation. Afterwards, she always came into the kitchen with me and Chummy. She had been with his father originally, and knew the county like the back of her hand. We'd sit at the kitchen table drinking tea and laughing like drains. She always said if West China was bad, I ought to have known East China and Pekin.

She even knew Boris. "That Boris Dawson! You really pick them, don't you, Peg? Now *he* was a character. As long as I've known him – and neither he nor I is any spring chicken, we went to high school together – he's had a young girl on a string and a big fat manuscript under his arm. Wonderful act that. Impress-a-girl, my brother used to call it. Did he ever get you in the sack?"

"Not quite."

"There but for the grace of nosy neighbours, huh? That was part of his act, too. I think he used to inform on himself just to keep the shotguns away. Funny world. If you knew him and Bob and Ron Macrae you'd know Art Fanshaw, then. Now he . . ."

And she was off. The odd time, I cracked out the whisky for her, but she was an alcoholic, still is, as far as I know, and she got beyond herself quickly. I've never had any head for the stuff myself and it was no fun trying to look after Chummy on weak legs, so I refrained, mostly.

It was almost an enjoyable convalescence, particularly after Chummy's neurologist had a look at Asher and said he'd been misdiagnosed, for there were some flus that simulated MS. He'd be fine, Dr Hughes said, if he stopped all his drugs, rested a while, then started jogging. And he was, eventually.

"Thought the young bugger was faking," Amabel said. (Ash's father was always "the old bugger" after she got to know me.)

"Oh, Amabel, the doctor said he had it."

"Gosh, I like you, Peg: thirty-eight years old and still shockable. That's something."

Somebody liked me: the idea went through me like fizzy ginger ale.

Tally, of course, was at the house a lot as well. I did not like him any better than at first. There are gossips and gossips: there was no malice in Amabel's outrageous news, but Tally, when he brought information, laid it at our feet twisted and lumpy and knotted with sinister prospects. When he came to tell Asher, for instance, that the riding's provincial Conservative association wanted him to let his name stand as candidate for the new election, he held the prospect out cringingly as if it was grisly meat for a hungry but unreliably ferocious dog. Asher sat bolt upright and began his recovery at once. My heart failed.

"Look at it this way, it will take his mind off his muscles," Amabel said. "And that kid."

"I wish you wouldn't call Chummy 'that kid.' "

"If I liked kids I would have had some. Peggy, it's time you faced the fact that Asher can't stand him."

Frankness is not always a virtue, Philip.

"Look," she said, softly because I was crying, "he wants this nomination and he wants it badly. He can afford it. I've been keeping his case work up and the juniors are doing just fine – everybody and his brother's going to law school now, you can get a genius for a dime – there's no reason he shouldn't run. But you've got to keep Chummy out of the picture. Stay out of it yourself, if you want. Asher may have private feelings about his son and heir, he's fond of him in his way, but he goes a lot by appearances, and he doesn't want to be seen – he doesn't want even to see himself – with that kid. I know, I know, he's your treasure, your crusade. He's just not all that beautiful though, and you'd better realize that."

For a moment, I hated her. But I knew she spoke the truth. I wish I'd cut out and run then, but of course I had no place to go.

There was another problem. I took Asher to task about it. "How could you possibly," I asked, "be a Tory?"

"Good God, woman, what else would I be? One of Maggie's flaming power-mad Liberals?"

120

"But, Asher, in the history books in school the Tories were the bad guys."

"Peggy, the depths of your naiveté are fathomless. What are your politics, then?"

I thought for a bit. It wasn't wise to mention, I thought, Aunt Frieda. Or even Uncle Stanley, now comfortably in his grave. Stu . . . wasn't it funny that Amabel was a cheerful drunk and Stu wasn't? "I don't know," I said. "I've never thought about it."

"Did you ever vote when you were in the convent?"

"The enumerators mostly missed us. I think they thought we were a sorority house. But we voted once, yes."

"Well, how did you vote?"

I thought back. When the enumerators came I had to go to Sister Mary Rose to find out all our worldly names. I remembered Mary Elzevir's was Emma Schwartz. I remembered our procession to the polls. We had been much divided whether we should commit this worldly act at all, but in the end, seven of nine of us went.

"CCF," I said.

I thought he was going to go purple with rage but he started to laugh and I started to laugh and we wound up staggering and gulping in each other's arms. "It was for the farmers," I gasped. "We voted CCF because it was good for the farmers."

That night he made love to me and I thought the bad years were over. Henceforward he referred to me as his proletarian wife, which was a shade better than saintly wife. More apposite.

With Tally, who was his campaign manager, we arranged a sort of separation of powers. I would not campaign with Asher, but I would not campaign against him. I would run the house smoothly, keep Chummy out of the way, and perhaps do a little volunteer work to help the family image.

I had come to know Asher well enough to be surprised when he won the election. *I* wouldn't have voted for him, but his own constituents flocked to him. Handsome is as handsome does meant nothing to them.

So, on the surface, for a number of years, we were a handsome political couple. Both devout Anglicans, you know, but unfortunately she spends all her time with her son, who isn't right. Isn't available for the bazaar. Odd-looking woman, quiet, but . . . I don't know: something about her not quite-quite.

Overheard that, I did, and said, under my increasingly vehement breath, "You bet."

Your visits were a comfort in those years, Philip. You were the only private friend I invited to the house after John moved west. I remember your enormous quiet invading the drawing room, so that for once I felt at ease in it.

Asher still went to church, but I did less and less. I had girls to help with Chummy by then, and of course they wanted Sundays off. Often, too, there were political brunches, horrid things. I'd have to get someone extra in to look after Chummy, organize the food while Asher was at early Mass at St Mary Magdalene's and then, already exhausted, play the hostess. I don't think I managed to wear quite the right things – for brunches you dress as for Christabel's cottage and I couldn't do it in my own house – but I got through them somehow, groggy from the champagne and orange juice, and Asher said they were useful.

When I went to church I went to evensong. I loved the old people's high quavering voices. They reminded me of home, the odd time we had a full-time minister and there was evening service and the very old went and faltered through "There were ninety and nine."

But I didn't go regularly and for an important reason: I had decided when Chummy was born that it was more useful to be an existentialist than to be a Christian.

Because you see, as a Christian, how could I accept Chummy except as a punishment, when I wanted him to be a blessing? "These things are sent to try us" is a useful sentence for getting through an unpleasantness; and in a way Chummy was an unpleasantness, but I did not think I could give him any happiness if I took him that way. And I had remembered a little of Husserl and Heidegger and Kierkegaard, I knew that an existentialist accepted existence and determined its quality in terms of his inevitable death. Knowing that Chummy's death was inevitable, that his life would end sooner than I was prepared to admit – because the doctors (and by now I had been through dozens of them) were adamant on the point that I was not to expect him to be normal, not to dream of a long life for someone whose expectations were rage and pain – I felt that it was only by rejecting, well, original sin that I could cope with him. He taught me to be, if not an existentialist, at least to cease to be Pelagian.

And he was a lovely child, Philip. When he wasn't upset because of pressure or pain, he was marvellous. He underwent tortures in the clinics asking only to hold my hand. I'd call him Pooh and we'd say we were friends, and do reading or co-ordination exercises in the waiting rooms. We formed play groups for other children and talked to the mums. Sometimes he was like a little wise old man.

Sometimes, too, he was feckless, wild. That was when Asher couldn't stand him. He must have felt he was a punishment for sins I was ignorant of.

For a while, then, we achieved an equilibrium. Asher was quite a successful politician – he has a brain, after all – and although he was not warm with his constituents, he was conscientious. So that he was happier, and because he was, we were.

Then Asher did a dreadful thing. He bought me Uncle Eddie's house for a birthday present.

He'd been away; I didn't know where, or much care. I was busy. He came back and packed us both in the car on my birthday and drove us smack down the French Line to Uncle Eddie's.

"I couldn't get your old place," he said, "and frankly I didn't think you'd want it. But I knew we needed a bolt-hole in the country, and while I was driving around I found this one. From the other side of the river. Will you look at that? I didn't know they had those ferries back in here. My God, it's wonderful. They don't use it now they've put the new bridge on the sixth line but here, take a look out this little window, isn't it a gem? You could fish for trout."

"Catfish," I corrected automatically. He didn't seem to hear.

The legend is that Eddie died while consorting with the lady who owned the antique store in the village. He was ninety, and a great weight by that time. By the time she wriggled out from under him she was in poor shape herself. He left her everything he owned, except the government pace maker, which was buried with him unless Tories are even worse than I think. She sold the house to Asher lock, stock and barrel and moved to Florida. I found two of Mother's pie plates in the kitchen cupboard.

I hated that house. If anything was a punishment for my sins, that was. Asher would arrive home all sprightly on a Friday night and I'd have to pack us all up for the long, long drive and we'd get there and I'd find myself scrubbing Eddie's table, cleaning Eddie's toilet, putting Chummy to bed in Eddie's spare room. Naturally, I got rid of the worst of Eddie's things, his crummy squares of blankets, his nasty sheets, even the enormous overalls he'd called overhauls. I got rid of his nasty flour sifter, his crusty cannister set, his corroded silver spoons that set my teeth on edge. I'd have got rid of the whole place, given any choice. But Asher loved it. He would scoop through cupboards, himself with the finest collection of blue and white Chinese porcelain in Toronto outside of the museum, and pull out a mouse-chewed rolling pin, a rusty Old Plug tin, a dog-eared notebook with Eddie's half-literate scrawl in it, "*Rat Pison today.*"

I wanted to paint it all white inside but Asher wanted it left as it was. Genuine Old Ontario, he said it was. You bet. Fortunately or unfortunately, walking along the road with Chummy one day (trying to keep him out of the fields so that grass seed and dandelion floss wouldn't plug his tube), I passed McCrory's place and there, hanging out the wash, was Tess.

"Well, I never," she said.

She was still black-eyed and good-looking. She'd married a

poet named Duff and they'd moved here to live off the land. Her father was dead, Billy lived in Sudbury, and her mother lived in the village.

I asked her if she was still called Treesa. I told her my husband called me Peg. I asked them over for a drink.

I never feel it's fair to associate the decline of my life with Tess, but she was certainly part of it. Ash said I was jealous of her, and perhaps I was. Her husband, whom she called Duffy, was one of the funniest story tellers I've ever heard. Ash used to bring Tally up with us, and we'd get Duffy and Tess over and put out a couple of bottles of malt scotch on the table and the fun would begin. Among the lot of them, they'd take the world apart. If my account is somehow prejudiced, it's because it was my world that they were taking apart.

Asher, naturally, had become interested in local history since he had become part of the provincial government; he was a minister without portfolio by then. Tess, naturally, knew it all because she was a McCrory; she knew all about my Uncle Walter the bootlegger and how he beat Aunt Millie with his blackthorn stick; she knew things I'd never heard about Uncle Doog and Auntie Mary. (She was a Presbyterian but she joined the United Church choir to get him, and apparently he had a girlfriend in Port Huron, Michigan, he went across to every Friday when he was supposed to be at the wholesaler's in Sarnia.) She knew all about the Macraes, that big United Church Mafia that ran the township, she called them, and she knew which Macraes drank behind the barn and which did their drinking right there in the kitchen with the blinds down. She told the story of Uncle Eddie and the widow woman in a kind of chorus with Duffy, and it was, indeed, hilarious. Somehow, I refrained from adding my childhood experience to it. I knew I was going to have to get into Eddie's deathbed with Asher and pretend I wanted to make love.

Weekend after weekend: Tally's tales of his old hometown in Ireland (it's remarkable how much of storytelling consists of revealing hypocrisy), Duffy's of Nova Scotia, of the Poets'

League in Toronto, Asher's imitations of my genteel discourse when I first came out of the convent. I sat there cringing, helping myself to the whisky, trying to take the pain away.

Tess grew bolder and bolder. Wasn't the whole of life hilarious? She went from the smell of suppressed sex in the convent school to the funny way Shirl and I always smelled a little of gasoline. She went from Grammacrae's glass eye that got turned around sometimes to, inevitably, my hilariously funny mother who was out in every kind of weather washing windshields, pumping gas, trying to make a go of a business everyone knew had failed twenty years before. "You should have seen her, Ri . . . Peg. You never got along with her, did you? There she'd be out in your father's old plaid shirt, and her glasses would get steamed up and she'd scrub away at those windshields as if they were the last ones on earth. She wore men's boots and I guess she even wore his pants towards the end. The minute a car went by she'd be out there, trying to wave the customers in. She used to make these awful signs: One Cent Less Here (Daddy used to say she couldn't cut two cents off, she'd a one-track mind). My God, in a storm, once she even got the old tow-truck going. We'd see the snow come and we'd say it was old Mother Heber shaking herself out of her feather bed."

I wanted to cry, but I couldn't. I wanted to hit Tess, but I couldn't. But that was the last time but one I ever went to that house.

That fall, Chummy took a turn for the worse. He'd always been prone to seizures, but they came more and more quickly. I knew what it meant, of course, but I was so proud of him, I loved him so much . . . and he was brave, Philip, and he'd just started a normal kindergarten class, which was a victory . . . I wouldn't let go. Both his specialists warned me what it meant, but I thought I could pull him through. I insisted on an operation that didn't help. When he came home, I nursed him day and night. Asher, who had grown fonder of him than I realized, often sat with both of us, reading *The Wind in the Willows* or *Winnie the Pooh*, hoping the child could hear.

But after that operation he receded from us. He spoke to us as if from very far away, and then he died.

I came home from his funeral and started making his supper. Asher watched me and said, "Were you ever happy with me?"

I looked up from the egg I was scrambling just so. "No."

"I'm going up to the country with Tally for a few days. Want to come?"

"No. Love to Tess." Which was automatic. I felt, obscurely, that her stories were payment for centuries of Protestant bigotry and I had to accept them, even in absentia.

On the Monday Chummy's doctor phoned Asher at the Parliament Buildings because I had gone to the clinic as usual. They sent me away somewhere for a rest.

When I got back, Asher said he thought we should separate for a while. I remember saying quite calmly, "You've found someone else, haven't you?"

He admitted, yes, he had. But she was very young. He wasn't sure, yet. She was lovely; he wasn't sure it was right to saddle her with all of his – our – problems.

"What's her name?"

"You may remember her; she worked in my last campaign: Katie Rogers."

My mind seemed very dull; perhaps it was the pills they had given me. I could grasp ideas one at a time, not as constellations. I remembered Katie Rogers, a tall girl who looked like an antelope but had long, nervous fingers. Yes, I thought, she's right for him, one of the classy ones who looked as if she could wear the world as easily as she wore her camel-hair coat on her shoulders; though of course she couldn't, not with those nervous hands.

"We could adopt her," I said.

"Peggy, I've led you a terrible life, I admit it. I've never been good enough for you. I want to set you free."

Couldn't he see that the last thing I wanted was to be free?

He talked more and more, but I didn't hear what he said. She was young and she needed him, things like that. A lot of words. All I could see in my mind was the cool, long-fingered, knotted hands of Katie Rogers.

In the end, Asher did set me free. He left, and I settled down to a little simple drinking, something I'd grown fond of. It swept away the pressures of the day. Tally walked in then, and suggested we go to bed and I said, sure. The next day, I got a hand-delivered lawyer's letter.

*   *   *

Stirling the starling no longer sits miserably on the telephone wire airing his armpits and thrusting his beard miserably into the wind, complaining in a shrill little voice before he bellyflops down to the pavement. He has learned to fly. I miss him, but only sort of.

The herons still stand, early in the morning, one-footed, on the estuary. When the sun gets high they disappear and the goofy bird begins, again, his spiralling. The field is still a world, but its grasses are drying and going to seed; it has a brownish cast; it has lost some of its magic. Ah, we all do, I say to it, but even the Stirlings learn to fly.

I used to think Stirling was really saying, I didn't choose to be a bird, I won't, I won't. He was a stumpy sort of bird, ill-shaped. Perhaps he was born with short wings and had to wait until they grew in. I'd sit there and look at him and say, I didn't choose either, Stirling, none of us did. We just have to put up with it, and some of us, like you and me, have nothing but a natural talent for complaining.

I don't know how long after I got the lawyer's letter it was that I woke up in Detroit, but when I woke up in Detroit I knew something bad had happened. I knew from the smell I was in Stu's printing shop and I know from experience that Stu is, for me, a kind of death wish. I had a huge, aching head and when I sat up I bumped it on the underside of a table.

"Now hurry on and get out, kid," I heard Stu say. "Get out before the help comes."

I hurried on, all right. I crawled out and washed in the big

128

horse-basin he has there (I can still remember the smell of the Snap) and looked at myself in the broken triangle of mirror that stands on the pipe over it and thought, girl, you are not what you once were. But I stood firm and combed my hair, checked my pockets, found my purse. Stu threw me my shoes.

"Next time," he said, "bring your own booze, kid."

It was cold for March. I knew where I was and even who I was, which seemed constructive under the circumstances. I walked in the grey dawn to the bus station and sat numb among the rubbies until the right bus came. I rode it up the river to the town Cousin Mel's ferry lands at. I wondered if the ferry still went, but it did, so I stood on it, the only foot passenger, holding onto its iron side, not thinking, not feeling, not knowing or wanting to know what I had been doing, until it shuddered to the other side.

"Where were you born?" the Immigration man said.

"Heberville," I said, and crunched up the gravel hill past the hardware store that became the antique lady's store and now seemed to sell macrame pots, up to the shoulder of the road, and then along it, south. Not looking. Not feeling.

A traveller in hats going to Wallaceburg took me the half mile south to the French Line. He looked sad, but it would be, to sell hats now.

The old road was the same, hunched into frozen ruts. There was no point in looking at any of the farms. They'd all changed hands but Peacocks'. Our place was half torn down, though the Esso oval hung crooked in the wind. Doog's and Mary's was looking better. The new people had given it a coat of paint. The Salada Tea letters were gone out of the window. I wondered if Asher had sweet-talked them away at last, for Katie.

The wind came straight from the north. I was wearing only a raincoat. I leaned away from it, slipping and sliding in the frozen ruts. Where the Orange Hall had been. An old piece of tow-rope lashing in the wind from a dead elm tree. Where the Laver kids (why didn't we ever play with them, even on the deadest summer days?) had had a swing.

129

Down the rubbly riverbank, across the stepping stones, up the other side (gash on one knee), frozen now, hands red and raw: good, key's where we left it. Inside.

I flicked the thermostat up high and threw myself on Uncle Eddie's bed.

I got up once, I remember, and went to the bathroom and changed into a nightie I found there, mine or Katie's. Then I went back to bed and slept like the dead again. I don't know how long.

When I woke up there was someone I'd never seen before sitting on a chair looking at me. He had little round eyes, little round glasses, a yellow beard and a little knitted cap on his head.

"Pennies from heaven," he said.

I lay very still. I don't remember being afraid, but I lay very still. "Who are you?"

"Oliver. Who are you?"

It seemed too complicated a question to answer. I closed my eyes and rolled over again. When I woke up he was thrusting a bowl of soup at me. It was made of lentils and vegetables and a lot of garlic. "Good for the lungs," he said.

"This is *my* house," I said weakly.

"You never owned a house," he said. "I can tell by the look of you. Move over."

Quick as a whip he pulled off his pullover and his jeans. Under them he was wearing Uncle Eddie's yellow long underwear I had stuffed into a cranny in the woodshed. He whipped that off. I thought of making some kind of protest, then I thought of the warmth of human flesh and things like being hanged for a sheep as a lamb, in for a penny out for a pound . . . pennies from heaven.

He said he was a carpenter. Well, take any hundred young men between twenty-eight and thirty-five you meet these days and twenty-five per cent will say they're carpenters. And he was doing carpentry work. He was doing something queer to the kitchen, upholstering it with the lumber Eddie had been saving in the shed since 1901, so that it looked like something out of "Woodstock Handmade Houses" without quite exorcising Eddie. But his real talent lay elsewhere. He was a revelation. With, of course, a small *r*.

That was a strange time, and I don't know how long it lasted. I mostly slept. The weather was bad. He cobbled away at the kitchen walls and made rooty soups. Then I'd hear him put down his tools and sigh and begin to unbuckle himself. I didn't think about anything. Whenever I began to think, I heard Stu's high whine, "Ash Bone, Ash Bone, you marry Ash Bone and come complainin' to me about it." Why think about Stu and Ash Bone when, as Treesa's Duffy used to say, there's something even better than good malt liquor around?

I won't say anything more about Oliver because I don't know anything more about him. He said Ash had told him to do the job. I knew from his accent he was an American, probably a draft dodger. He seemed about thirty. He could, as he said, hammer some. And he hammered pretty well at me.

Then one day he said, "We need some money."

"Money?" I said sleepily.

"Money," he said. "Bread."

I wobbled lazily across the room and found my purse. I had $6.97. "There should be ten dollars in the sugar bowl," I said.

"What do you think we've been eating on all these days?"

"That's all the money I've got. You can get some bread for that."

"Look, I need money, real money. He's never paid me anything for that job."

"You'll have to ask him."

"Can't you write me a cheque? Haven't you got a joint account?"

I looked for my cheque book but I remembered I'd sent it to Ash's lawyer.

"That all you've got?"

"We had a falling out," I said lamely.

His voice began to sound ugly. "You mean you're not even speaking to the guy?"

"I don't know."

"Well, you better go back and see: we need bread."

I began to gibber a little and he shook me. "I don't even believe this is your house, lady."

I was scared for a moment, scared like a child in the dark and he must have seen it. He leapt out of bed and began to button himself into Eddie's ludicrous underwear (he was about the size of an elf and I often wonder if I dreamt him) and pulled on his jeans, his sweater, his work boots. Then he did a little dance like Rumpelstiltskin and began to scream about the world being full of decadent capitalists, vile deceivers. He sounded like a bad parody of Stu. I lay back astounded.

"Even you," he yelled, "you're a phony."

A phony what? I wondered.

I heard him throwing his tools in his box. I heard him leave. I stretched and went back to sleep. I was full of his revelation.

He took Asher's ten-speed bicycle.

There were no lights at Tess and Duffy's. I recalled Duff had a Canada Council grant to go somewhere exotic. I waited for Oliver to come back, but he didn't, so I rummaged around and found things to eat, jars of rice and beans I'd stored away from the mice, tins of pâté and salmon and tuna fish. I lived there for quite a long time like a fugitive, like a robber, the curtains tight shut at night, myself hidden in that bed like a pea in a pod, until the weather got better. Then I began to sneak outside a little and weed the borders, tidy the winter's muck away. I put the rocking chair on the porch. Once I even went to the store for some bread. They weren't surprised to see me.

Then one day Amabel Webster drove up and I knew that it, whatever it was, idyll or nightmare or dream, was over.

"Is this where you've been all the time?" she asked in her harsh kind voice. "I didn't know where the hell you were, we've been looking all over, Asher's mad as hops, there are rumours and he doesn't want to call the police, we called everyone you knew, we even called your brother, nice guy, your brother, said he hadn't seen you since 1964, then last winter you came and drank all his booze. Ash came up here and looked after you first went, you must have come here later, huh? Then about four days ago, just before the weekend, this little guy with a beard comes roaring into my office and starts a song and dance about Asher owing him money for work on his house – my God, isn't that something? Ash'll be fit to be tied – and after half an hour we got it out of him it was this house and you were here."

"Did you give him any money?"

"Asher didn't want to, said he wasn't responsible for work you'd ordered."

"I didn't. Order it, I mean."

"Well, I got rid of him for a hundred bucks."

I laughed. I hadn't laughed for a long time. Laughter is fatal in bed. "He took Asher's ten-speed, too."

"Where'd you find him?"

"He was here already."

"My God, isn't that something. I must tell my crook of a nephew. You move into somebody's house, work on it, screw some money out of them. Was he a good lay?"

"He was all right."

"Well, listen, kid, you're in trouble. You've got to pack up and come in to town with me now."

I shook my head. "I can stay here, Amabel."

"No, you can't. He may have bought it for your birthday but he's never given you the papers."

"He never gave me the papers to anything."

"Well, if you come in to town with me now you'll get something. He's got to give you something."

"I'm all right here, Amabel."

"No, you're not. He'll have you out quick as a wink. He hates you now."

"He always did."

"Look, I'm not here to dissect his character, I've known him longer than you: he has this fatal male flaw, he likes his pullets tender so they can't answer back. You made a fool of yourself with Tally, you went around to Katie's with that knife, you're in for it now, come back and face the music." Amabel is fond of clichés.

"It was only a grapefruit knife."

"It was a knife."

I stared at her, through her. "I think I'll stay here."

"What'll you live on, grass?"

"I'll be all right, Amabel."

"If you're all right what are you doing mending Chummy's clothes?"

The space between that house and this house is best filled, Philip, by telling you to look at the hell-paintings of Hieronymous Bosch. I went back with Amabel. I went to court for something called an Examination for Discovery, which is the worst piece of gynaecology I have been through. In the course of this I discovered that I had been a slut, a whore, and a madwoman: that I had protected my son's life at the cost of my husband's career, harboured political enemies among my friends, and, worst of all, failed to hold my liquor. If it had not been for Amabel's pointing out that I had also failed to hire my own lawyer, I would have been thrown out on the street.

"You *must* know a lawyer," she thundered at me. I was busy drinking her whisky and it was hard to think. "You know lots of people, he kept sending you to take courses, remember?"

"They weren't law courses."

"Think, girl, think. Somewhere in your head, somewhere in that scrambled egg you have for a brain, is a lawyer."

Bellman Hibbert had thinned out and looked positively dashing. He rubbed his hands. "My God, I've been dying to get my hands on Ash ever since he became deputy minister." I pointed out that I wasn't dying to get my hands on Asher. "You'll want something," he said.

"The house in the country."

"Really? You told Mother you hated it."

"That's right. I hate it. I'd forgotten that."

"Rita, you're not well."

"I'm worn out, they keep chasing me, I have to run."

"You need a place to sit still now."

134

"No, I have to run. They'll give me Chummy back if I run fast enough. And I can't, I can't."

Asher wanted to sign me into the Clarke Institute but Bellman wouldn't let him. "Once he signs you in, God knows if you'll get out," he said. I couldn't live with Amabel any more, not now the lines were drawn up. I couldn't work, I couldn't collect my head together, I couldn't cross the road. Bellman and Maggie found me a room and Dr Stern. They wouldn't let me take any of Chummy's things with me. I told them they were cruel.

Asher moved a lot that year. I used to go wherever he was living and sit under his window and cry.

Sometimes I drank and went out and tried to pick up men. I thought, maybe it will be like Oliver, I didn't know Oliver, maybe his name wasn't even Oliver, but it was good. I should have been married to Oliver. But all I could find were drunks and once I found a bad one, and Dr Stern said I had to stop or he'd lock me up.

I said I wouldn't mind being locked up. I'd been locked up all my life, what was the difference, and then he said, "But I thought you were happy with the Eglantines," and I cried and cried.

He was a lovely man, Dr Stern, Philip, though not a Christian. We had long philosophical conversations on days when my mind was not jumping around. At first I thought he reported to Asher or Bellman, but he convinced me finally that he reported to no one. I think I tried to convince him he ought to report to God but in the end he led me to some kind of reason, and I am grateful now.

We made up a kind of Rule, including the Thou Shalt Nots. I gave up baying under Asher's window, or trying to phone Katie. I went once a week to Chummy's grave. I wanted to work with children, but we decided I should not. I got up at a decent hour, went to Dr Stern, had a proper lunch, and came home and read. I went to the movies in the evening if I could find a non-violent one. I gave up going to bars. Making an exhibition of myself, as Asher's lawyer put it.

Still, inside me, there's a rebellious soul who wishes she'd told more on the mountain. Who wishes she had not given up reading the papers regarding the Rise of Asher Bowen. Who wishes she had gone to the wedding of Asher Bowen and Katie Rogers. Who wishes she had actually sent the wedding-note to Katie that said, "I wish you joy of Uncle Eddie's bed."

But, oh well, what's the use of wondering why things happen, what's the use of grieving? The birds fly high. I never converted Dr Stern, nor did he quite convince me that life was a bundle of joy (how could he when I knew well he was a man standing in a consulting room full of emotional guts and excrement?) but we came to a kind of understanding with me, with the person I am now. Bellman traded Asher's freedom for this lovely house and its view and Mr Macdonald and his boxes of groceries.

Dr Stern didn't think that was right. He thought I should be energetic and independent. Sometimes he sounded like someone out of Samuel Smiles. But I said I was sick of striving . . . to be a better Christian, to be a better girl. "They make you walk one more step until you drop," I said. "I want to sit a while."

Asher wanted me out of the province. I don't blame him.

Just before I left, I tried to see him, tried to make peace with him. I wanted to apologize for some of the things I'd done. I guess, too, I wanted to be apologized to. The only one who'd see me was Tally, who shook his head. "He pretends you're dead," he said. "He's set against you now. He won't see you and if you try to see him or Katie it'll be lawyers again. I'm sorry, Peg."

"You should be."

Tally looked at me steadily "Asher's my best friend," he said. "Men are loyal."

I did good things, too, last year, Philip. I went to group therapy sessions, where I discovered my miseries were less than others'. I went to all kinds of meetings. "If you can't find a movie, find a meeting," Dr Stern would say. I went to theosophical meetings, philosophical meetings, meetings about women, about the weather. I went to the annual meeting of the Karma Co-Op, a General Motors shareholders' meeting, Friends of the Yorkville Library meetings, and, once, with someone I met at Group, a Presbyterian church supper.

I went to a lot of Women's Liberation meetings; no, I shouldn't capitalize the words, because they were never the same group twice. Some of them preached to women that they should have pride in themselves. Some said that all men were homosexuals at heart and that all women should be lesbians, a gospel I do not support. At these I wanted to shout, "We must love one another or die." I'm still appalled by the thought of a segregated world, I suppose, as I'm appalled by the sex-hate of the early Christians, of my early self.

I went to court. I thought I'd have a chance to play Joan of Arc, but I was obedient to Bellman, said what I'd been told to say, and was divorced in two minutes, costs to the other side. I heard someone say at a party not long after, "Tally should've been ashamed of himself for that put-up job; she'd have bust out six weeks later anyhow, they all do eventually." I got a piece of paper that said I belonged to myself again. I should have been sad but I wasn't. I was relieved. It was over.

So I sit on this shore. Empty. Alone. I don't pick up men any more. I don't drink. I read a bit. I watch the birds. Sometimes a ship goes by. It's nice here.

John came, the other day. I was surprised. He said he'd had a heck of a time getting my address from Asher. He had to threaten to ask it out loud in church. It's good to see John with an impish smile on his face. He's married again. Michael's in graduate school, doing philosophy even though there won't be an academic job open in Canada until 1990. We went for a walk down the shore and decided not to talk about our grievances with the world. God knows, he says, where Christabel is. He hopes she's well. He's teaching out west, has tenure, likes it. His wife has four kids and teaches fine arts.

We couldn't help talking, though, about our early selves, our foolishnesses. We were, we decided, worms struggling blind out of our country world, trying to grow eyes. It's painful to grow eyes, and it even hurts other people. We did what we could to, let's say, adjust to our society. As our parents did. It isn't as easy as storybooks tell us it is. There are more kinds of people than they prepare us for. More ways of being, fortunately in the end, than we at first know how to see.

We talked, of course, about my funny chasing after philosophy. How Pascal always puts us both to sleep. How people always sing "Amazing Grace" out of tune. I talked about the Elders in the Temple and he told me about Auntie Frieda's making him stand on corners selling Trotskyite newspapers when he was living with her, until one day he got so embarrassed he wet his pants at Spadina and College and a policeman had taken him home and told Frieda not to do that to him any more. I told him about Uncle Eddie and why I had hated the house. We laughed and laughed about that and it did something for me.

He had to go away and give a speech at a university, but he came back. He said he hadn't driven all the way from the prairies to come for a cup of tea. He stayed four days and we walked when the tide was out and waded when it was in. Sometimes he had one sock to take off, sometimes two. He's just the same to look at, dim-eyed and red-haired. He told me about Christabel's unimaginable promiscuity, I told him about Mr Laidlaw and the Eglantines.

He told me something about the Bowens I'd never known: Asher's mother was mad. Which accounts, I suppose, in retrospect, for many things. If you want to account for anything.

I told him about Tess McCrory's stories. He said, with a wink, "Well, they were Catholics, you know," and we roared. There's no point checking back on the lives of the dead, but he said he had heard McCrory ran cockfights in his barn. But that was from his father, who was notorious for his lies.

We talked about living, about dying, about God. He asked me what I was going to do, and I said, "Why, sit right here. I'm a lily of the field, didn't you know?" He wasn't any more impressed than Dr Stern. He said that a good existentialist measures his life in terms of his death, which means he ought to hustle and get something done. I said my life always fell apart when I was a Martha and not a Mary. I wanted to sit here and be.

"There's winter to think of."

"Macdonald will bring wood."

"If you're a true Pelagian, you'll have to do something about yourself."

"I've been cured of Pelagianism. I believe in grace."

"And here it's abounding?"

"At least not hair-splitting."

But he went on at me like a true Heber, telling me I was living on ill-gotten gains, preaching self-sufficiency and self-improvement. In the end, I laughed. "Look," I said, "all over North America there are hordes of women my age trying to find jobs to support either their own consciences or their kids. I don't need to; therefore I am not doing that. It has been given to me to live in a house on the seashore and read and think, and that is what I am doing."

"And you're going to do it until you die?"

"Unless some other choice is made for me, yes."

"If your husband had not been a politician, if your son had been normal. . . ."

"There would have been another fate."

"But that's what I mean," he said. "You keep talking about fate. Nothing prevents you from walking to the ferry tomorrow. Nothing prevents you from coming out west with me."

"Nothing?"

"What did you sign away, then?"

"The privilege of living in Toronto or engaging in Ontario politics."

"That's corrupt!"

"Only if I want to live in Toronto or engage in Ontario politics, of which I have seen and heard quite enough."

John drew with his toe on the sand again. He has long white

toes. I thought, I wouldn't like them in bed. "Asher's an authoritarian jerk," he said.

"You're telling me that?"

"You've given in to the enemy."

"Peace has a price. I don't get to wet my pants handing out Trotskyite pamphlets."

"Do you want to do that?"

"No. I don't like authoritarians of any stripe."

"Well. So you're going to sit here until you're an old, old woman, not waging the wars of society, but collecting for ten years of bad sex."

"That's a man's way of putting it. Maybe even the right way of putting it. But I say I'm practising the negative virtues. I do no harm, here, to the world. I'll read my Penguin classics and go grey."

He rocked on his haunches. "I don't like it. I don't like it."

"You're the philosopher. You should."

"Yes. Socrates would be pleased with you."

"I'm even pleased with myself."

"Do you remember the last time I saw you?"

"At the funeral, wasn't it?"

"God, no; it was last year. We met in Toronto. You tried to take my pants off."

"I used to do that sort of thing."

"Didn't you honestly remember?"

I remembered that I did remember and had wanted to hide the memory. I had to be honest.

"You said that if you didn't find someone to care for, or someone who cared for you, you would let yourself die."

"It's not that easy. And I'm better now."

"I'm glad."

I could tell he still thought I was wrong, but I was glad he had come, glad he had cared to come. He even offered to sleep with me, though he made it clear it was a service; he was happy with his wife and hadn't much taste for anyone else. I said that that rage had finally gone away. I didn't want anyone I didn't care for, except the mysteriously efficient Oliver, who was

140

somehow classic. There's apparently a greed for sex that comes and goes.

Before he left he told me something I didn't know. My sister Shirley has been trying to get in touch with me. Anything sent to Asher is returned marked "Address unknown" but she wrote to John, who decided to track me down. She is not, as Stu said, divorced and on welfare. She is still perfectly happy and living in Texas.

"Funny Stu lied to me."

"Haven't you found out yet the world is full of liars?"

"Like black Hebers and red Hebers?"

"The black ones were the ones Grammacrae cast her evil eye on."

"Funny, I never thought she liked me, but I came out beige."

"You have the gift of unlosable innocence: it's a rare one."

"It's a form of lazy naiveté, really."

"It used to be called virtue."

Here was someone again accusing me of being virtuous. I argued with him a bit. "I've made a lot of trouble for people, John."

"I'm sure you have. But remember, the world's full of bastards. If you don't, you'll find yourself another one."

"Here?"

"More likely Macdonald drunk and horny than Sir Lancelot. So you're determined to stay?"

"Is there a better place to live a godly, righteous, and sober life?"

"You could do what your bishop asks."

"I'm through with doing, John. I told you that."

He drew a little picture in the sand with his long white toes. It was a mermaid. "Pelagia's a false cognate of Marina who is Aphrodite," he said. "I read that in the *Penguin Dictionary of Saints.*"

"Somebody ought to write a thesis on how the Canadian mind diverges from the American mind because of Penguin books."

"Watch it, you're getting active. I've got to go, Rita."

We ambled up to the house. He put his bag in his car, ready to join the procession for the next ferry, or the one after that.

"I'm glad you came," I said.

"I am too. Write to Shirley."

"Oh yes. Blood is thicker than. . . ."

"Yeah. Don't freeze, here."

"No. Love to Bonnie. . . ."

"Sure . . ."

"And Michael . . ."

I hate partings. So does he. He drove off. I found an odd sock under his bed.

I went down on the beach and slept on a little Socrates for a while. Then I came back and wrote to Shirley. Almost by return mail a letter came full of curly goshes and gollies and snapshots. Her children are grown up. She wants me to come down. Well, I can't, but I'll ask her here. Meanwhile I think of her as a Good Heber in Good Texas, the part we associate with musicals and cowboys and generosity. If Shirl's there, it's sure to exist.

I thought about the family for a while when I put her letter away. It doesn't strike me it's any meaner than any other; it's just that because we lived in the country, isolated from distraction, we picked each other over like monkeys, knew each other inside out. I mean, who in Amabel's family knows or cares that she drinks? How did the Bowens hide Asher's mother's condition? The bunch of us were like apartment dwellers in West China, jammed against each other's front doors, with nothing but icy fields between. We couldn't go to the bathroom without all the others knowing. Every family has its blacks and reds, but not every family knows.

Stu, though: Stu was always a good man trying to be bad. I should write to him. Give him something to gnash his teeth against. He could use Dr Stern.

You know, Philip, I thought being with Dr Stern might lead me to some big mystical experience. I guess I'd read too much Jung. But it didn't; he was a logician. I don't remember much of what he did, except let me cry a lot, but when he really got me working on myself, what he did was lay out reality like a deck of cards, so that instead of the mysterious id, I was contemplating what was; not what had been, not what should be, but what was.

And I guess that's why I have to turn down your offer now, Philip. I was forty-two years old yesterday and I am just beginning to look at what is. I use the word "contemplate" to mean that, not as the expression of a mystical attempt to achieve oneness with God, or Buddha-hood or the Tao. *Rosa Eglanteria* is a small, five-petalled pink rose, just that. The field is a field that a variety of plants grow in. A variety of birds nest in the plants and feed off the insects that live among the plants. The seacoast has an ecology of its own. The birds have names and functions, as do the gastropods and the cockles and the mussels. I want to live here where a paved road is a paved road, a heron is a heron. I want the bread on my table to be bread, not money, not something fattening, not the Body of Christ. I have been offered a unique experience: the freedom to see things as they are. I can walk down this road to Mac Moan's listening not to the Nazis whispering in underground streams, but to birds and telephone wires and my own crunching steps.

I do not, in other words, wish to see eternity. I wish, for once, to see the here-and-now.

Rita, Pelagia, Peggy, Peg: I left the world before I had had a chance to discover it. When I had a chance to find it again, I sidestepped truth in the arms of Asher, who wanted a partner for a dance I'd never dreamed. When reality hit me in the face, I hid again.

Finally, I've acquired a taste for it. Macdonald, for instance, told me the other day that my goofybird/windhover is a spiralling snipe. It didn't bother me. I was tempted to run to the dictionary, mind you, to search for the symbolical connotations of the snipe, but I didn't. A snipe is a long-beaked marsh bird who amuses himself by spiralling into the sky and whistling with his wings. He is spotted, brownish, uxorious, and edible, though protected on this continent, I hope.

I don't, like some philosophers, disapprove of mysticism. I don't disapprove of your scheme to re-form the Eglantines. But, knowing I am imperfect, knowing also that I am part of the universe and entitled to be so, I wish to spend this part of my life seeing what I can see of the universe as it is, rather than attempting the perfecting of my soul. That is a worldly aim, Philip, but I need to be worldly.

Once I hunted in the hearts of roses for what I was to be. I tried to be a rose. The knight who plucked me found he could not bear my thorns. Then the roses reached out and robbed me.

Now I'm the crazy lady by the shore. That is what I want to be. No mystic, gnostic, hermetic, self-flagellating solitary anchoress; but a woman living by the shore. She reads a lot. Gets a little mail. Walks (but not naked; what would the locals think?) a little when the tide is out. Plays solitaire, thinks, not about her loss, but about her gain: this world, this finally painless life.

By all means open Eglantine House again, Philip. With Mary Pelagia's – my – blessing. But without me. I'm not the strong vessel you need; the pitcher that goes oftenest to the well may be cracked, all right, but its lifespan depends on where the cracks are. Mine are crucial and deep: I won't do.

Open your house again, Philip. There must be a hundred women who would love to retreat from their noisy, empty lives to the cloister and fill it once more with roses. But leave me here, please, to dream my redemptive dreams.

All my love, your grace,
Rita Bowen.

Envoie

Eglantine House creaks around me. Soon it will be dawn. What an act of indiscipline to stay up all night reading my own letter. How I enjoyed the writing of it! And some of the feeling came back to me as I read it tonight. I could smell salt on the wind.

How I love night. How I love loneliness. I have given them up again for a while. When I feel hypocritical about being sister superior I shall be able to remind myself that it is a mortification to return here as Martha, when I so much wanted to be Mary. I let Philip and Anthony persuade me; in the end I had no more arguments against them. I strained at the gnat and caught the fly again. I hope to God, I hope that with the help of God, I have done the right thing, that a good deed is not corrupted utterly by my lack of faith.

It must be warm down there on the seacoast again. I could be reading, beachcombing. The old men will be raking the sand for Irish moss again, drying it on the road. It was so beautiful there. . . .

But by midwinter the view of the Pelagian shore was reduced to the size of a palmprint on a frosted window pane. The house creaked and groaned in the Maritime gales. The county kept forgetting to plough as far as my house, Mr Macdonald became dilatory. I, who had resolved to meditate on the possibilities of life, became involved in a duel with his adversary, death. I had to move a couch into the kitchen, the rest of the house was unbearably cold, and feeding wood to the monstrous furnace took all my energy. I began to meditate on death.

Life, I decided, is a sentence between brackets: these brackets must be seen to contain what is, not what might have been. It is useless to ponder on what might have been, but entirely proper to map the future in terms of the real past. While I was writing to Philip, I had, in the intervals between the sentences, written a great deal more, truth and untruth, in my head, on the sky, on the evanescent clouds. I had assigned myself the winter for pondering what should be done with that part of the sentence that remained before the brackets must inevitably close. With my shoulders swathed against the drafts in every piece of cloth I could find in the house, and my feet in the oven, I found that I wanted that end bracket to come fast.

I was reading, I recall, one of the Europeans; someone I had acquired by mail, in translation, from a New York remainder house. E. M. Cioran, I think. He seemed, at any rate, to be a Manichean. His view of the world was not optimistic; his meditations on suicide were profounder than what he had to say about life. I shivered. I knew what he meant.

In a fundamental way, I felt, my life was over; I had run through a long span and had seen a good deal more history than was allowed people four or five hundred years ago. If, in fact, what we call the natural processes had been allowed to hold sway, I should already be dead: I should not have survived Chummy's birth. Spiritually, I decided, I was a fake and a failure. If my faith had been true, I should never have left Eglantine House. In my encounter with the world, I had failed profoundly to add anything to the equality of life. In fact, judged by any moral standards, any at all, I had soiled both the world and myself.

I could blame some of my misbehaviour, indeed, on Asher, who did not treat me well; and certainly some on Chummy's defect, which neither Asher or I were able to accept. But blame was never a virtue and if I were to follow the painfully acquired advice of Dr Stern and the morality of the Christians who raised me and sheltered me, I must take the failure of my life on my own shoulders and carry it whether I wanted to or not.

I did not want to carry it far, I decided.

It was winter, a winter deeper and bleaker than anything I had seen except at home perhaps; but no, the gale off the sea shut me in the way the winds at home had never done. And there was nowhere to go if I went out in it: I had purposely not made friends at the store or with the neighbours. I was as isolated as the Desert Fathers at noonday in their sandy lairs, though they never had to stoke a furnace to keep the pipes from freezing: or thaw them. I learned how to do that, too.

Death, I thought; why are we so afraid of it? Death is rest; for a real Christian, reunion. (Though I did not think of heaven; Asher would go to heaven and I never wanted to see him again.) (And besides, Hell is warm.) Death. We want more death, not less, in spite of what the papers say. We want to eat lots of cholesterol, stop purchasing time with vitamins, move ourselves out of the way to make room for others. The world is overpopulated. People are living too long. There are no jobs. The thing to do is to get people to die early, not retire early. Move along, move along, move to the back of the bus, mind the doors, keep the queue moving.

Men are angry with women; men are afraid of women. Women live longer than men, but why? Once the trauma of childbirth is outlived, they go on forever.

But what do they go on to? I asked, listening to my pipes, my plumbing. What have I to look forward to?

A selfish view, but a human one.

Eternity, I thought, eternity, hysterectomy, mastectomy:

from here, the operating table: the avoidance of the inevitable. You go so far, then the nodules grow inside you instead of the babies, the new life is cancerous, the doctors treat you with knives and poison gas, but in the end, the rule must be obeyed: the last bracket is there. Accept, I told myself, accept. You are here to die.

I thought of Asher; middle-age for him is the ascendant; power is within his grasp. Therefore male in the ascendant reaches to female in the ascendant – forty to twenty – to perfect his brackets. Biologically, he is right.

Biologically, I thought, I am over. Finished.

I have read women's journals of their middle age. They claim to be happy. The rages of romance, of sex, of childrearing, are over. They are free of the moon.

Soon, too, I shall be free of the moon.

And feared and scorned more than ever.

For if there is someone who is hated more than an awkward but intelligent young woman, it is a mature woman. Who can no longer be dismissed as subject to the moon. The suspicion of matriarchy is stronger even than the hostility to nubile youth. It is only kind, then, to get out of the way, isn't it?

Evil thoughts occurred to me, evil malicious thoughts. They must dispose of women, I thought: they want it that way. We must give them their heads: this is what they want, a world free of women who are past their nubile best, who are capable of thinking, who can direct them, who bring guilt and repression to the world. Women brought sin, they believe that, their hearts and their balls believe it, they act it out every day of their lives, treating their daughters like toys and their wives like encumbrances. Therefore let them get rid of women.

But to teach them something, not just their women, but all women.

I shall leave, I thought, the method up to them. They are so good at it.

I shall merely design the plot for them. I shall go further, much further than *Lysistrata*.

What age shall we aim for? Forty-five, I thought, three or four more years would suit me well enough: then I shall be

148

freed of merciless fantasies of mastectomy. That would be enough. Yes, I never nursed Chummy, he was having tests and operations; it's women who didn't nurse who get it, old maids, nuns, biological decadents like me. If I go at forty-five I'll get out of it.

And the others? Some take joy in grandmotherhood, but most of my generation have been discarded by this age; a whole generation is out there, earning, working to put the children through school, collecting maintenance until they're eighteen, but when that's gone, what? The routine job, pensionless, then the routine old age: soft toast and tea on seventy dollars a month: the government-sponsored operation: that's what is offered me. If I were not shut up like Mrs Rochester, Macdonald my Grace Poole, because of Asher's political position, I, too, would have that to live for, that only. Underpaid office slavery, poverty, mutilation, death: a generation of female bums, gentlemen, is in the wings.

Or will they go to live with their daughters as unpaid domestic help?

Forty-five might be the good age, I thought, perhaps fifty. To give them (me) a few years on their own, a space to think in, before the inevitable.

But if this project is to do good, to set an example, would that be the best age? The greatest good for the greatest number must be kept in mind. This is a moral country, politicians thunder this at us every day: our project must teach, gentlemen.

What would it teach women? That life, when the brackets are short, is worth something. When the number of days is limited, the days have value, just as money is of value to the poor in a way that it never is to the millionaire. A boy with a dollar is a singing bird compared to a Rockefeller of fifty. So let art be long, let life be short, for us.

For them? Let them be the ones who take life.

But if they are to learn anything?

Let them take it early. Let them breed on their women, but let every birth be a death. Then they will learn how women live.

149

And let every woman who has not given birth be gone at thirty.

They will bring the children up by themselves; they will learn the true quality of life from their children; particularly from their mistakes with children; especially from loving children, from weeping over children. The ones who are caring for children will learn the mercilessness of the ones who are not caring for children, who do not understand what living can be about, who have not seen love and hate and destruction and weariness in the nakedness of fear and exhaustion. Yes, let them do it. Let them get rid of us.

There will be no more mothers, no more grandmothers; no aunts, no female slaves. Nothing but good fresh fucks whose day is over on parturition.

They will have got what they want. And they will see what it is, their hunter's dream.

Asher, I thought, from his high righteousness, Asher alone can legislate this true casting down of golden crowns. Asher shall hold up the flaming sword, Asher shall be the one elected for this destruction.

They know what it is to kill the spirit. Let them kill the flesh: cleanly and properly, not by slicing it off an inch at a time, extracting humid receptacles, pulling out veins, hacking, slashing. Let them, instead of listening to our telephone calls, come and do a proper job of it.

There will be no old flesh. No chin whiskers to disgust them, no disfigured bodies to turn into guilt, no unseemliness. Only young women.

Think what it would do for the employment situation, for the pension plans!

We should die more, I thought, holding my hot hand to the frozen window pane to procure myself a view of the snow-wracked estuary, the gale. We should die more, we should die eagerly. Let us be battery hens: they will value us, then.

It was midwinter. The pipes had thawed, the pipes had frozen. It was true I did not work, but I had learned a great deal about keeping furnaces going. I was reading a little and thinking a lot, with my feet in the oven of the Keemac stove, wondering if they would bring it more oil even if the road was not open. With my hand and my hot breath and a vision of men doing work, not ordering it done, but men doing women's work as well as men's – as women are, with hope of no reward but cancer and toothless gums and toast, if they lived our lives. . . .

And I was more fortunate than most: that was what defeated me. I had a roof, though a draughty one, and a blackmailing sort of future, and a hope or two: I was Asher's hostage to fortune, he would keep me forever, here, the first Mrs Rochester, as long as he was in politics and there were things he feared I could tell. Bellman Hibbert had made sure of that. In exchange for my draughty winters, I would have lyric summers; there would always be food; I belonged to the old order, I had asserted my dower rights.

But the others?

Where do the discarded go? There is not work enough for all.

Death, I thought. Death is the friend. It is not Christian to say that, but it is true. If only it were easeful: there's the rub.

But they have always found a way, a way to what they want: a feed, a fuck, a death: they always get it. They will find a way. They run the world. They know.

Little ripe apples, once they are past their day what good are they?

Slice them off.

What good is a diamond in the soul if there is no God?

There will be no patient women, I decided for Asher. There will be only the young, perfect, underripe. There will be room then for all the hunters, and truths they have never had to know.

If you had been granted only twenty-five years, I thought, Pelagia, how long would you have danced?

I did not dare to ask Theresa.

I stood at the window and stared at the storm. They will be rid of us, I thought; they will spend a generation without us, two, three. Will they have learned?

I caught my breath: I was banking, finally, on some kind of

ending to the plan; on limitations; somewhere in my black, angry, jealous heart there was still room for a small eternity: a resurrection.

Then a little red car came skittering over the snow and almost slid into the side of the house: Brother Anthony.

To whom, about my theory, I did not, for a long time, speak.

For a strange moment, seeing him with a beard covered with rime, I thought he was Oliver.

"Anthony Stone," he gasped as I let him in, "from his grace."

"Whose grace?"

"Philip Huron."

"Good Lord. You're frozen. I'll make tea."

"You've found a fine and private place."

I moved my armchair away from the stove a little; set him down in it. Gave him soup and tea. The furnace started a clanging in the pipes. By the time I came upstairs from feeding it he was looking almost thawed. He opened his briefcase and handed me a letter from Philip, who introduced him as Brother Anthony Stone, possessor of a Canada Council grant to work on the history of the Protestant monastic establishment in Canada. I had a faint and interesting *frisson* that the future I did not believe in was on the menu.

He stayed perhaps three weeks, perhaps four. He was good company. When he had gone I missed him terribly. It was he who changed my mind.

We argued a lot. He was clever. When I said I was no longer a Christian in the orthodox sense, that I had rejected original sin when Chummy was born, that I had refused then and would always refuse to believe that either his infirmity or his death were part of the Divine Will, that I would not subscribe to a view that God was cruel, he had a battery of arguments for me. I said that if I were to be a Christian at all again I would have to be a Pelagian, a pure Calvinist, and believe that I was one of the non-elect, a justified sinner like the one in the book; instead of blaming my troubles on a wicked God (and surely

152

God was wicked if He created hydrocephalic children) I must at least pretend that I stood outside the crowd staring in the window.

I do not remember Anthony's arguments but they were both compassionate and efficient. They did not attempt to get around the fact that evil things had befallen me; they did not allow me to blame my misfortunes on God or on myself or on other people; they allowed for the spaces between the lines of the stave of logic, but they were logical in themselves; they made me feel that the religion that had sustained me was perhaps within my grasp again; they made me feel better.

While he was with me, he had his own rituals to perform. We got the Franklin stove in the livingroom working; he slept there, and at regular intervals performed his orisons. He did not ask me to join him, and I never did, though I went one Sunday to a country church with him. I didn't like it. The people stared at us. They weren't used to outsiders in the winter, and they knew I was the crazy lady from down by the sea.

We did not talk as much theology as I had expected. I suppose he looked into the abyss of my cluttered mind and dismissed the idea. He wasn't interested in theories, he said, he was interested in facts; sounding more than he knew like Dr Stern.

The fact that was uppermost in his mind was that he and Philip had decided to re-open Eglantine House and in order to do so they needed a sister who had previously belonged to the Order.

"Listen," I said, "you can't catch me. I told Philip that, at length. I'm not even a proper Christian. . . ."

"Listen," I said, "the Eglantines were a pretty piece of pseudomediaevalism; they'd make a nice chapter in the history if you wrote it right – not as kinky as Brother Ignatius and his colleagues in Wales, but, well, amongst all that plainness and dedication, decorative. But they aren't relevant for me any more, or for you either. They don't belong in the nineteen seventies."

He failed to take offence.

"Listen," I said, "devotional literature is all very well, poetry is magnificent, T.S. Eliot is still wonderful, but when you dissect most of it – think of Donne's 'Nor ever chaste, except You ravish me,' look at John Henry Newman, read your Hopkins – underneath the skin there's a fanatical kind of masochism; I won't have anything to do with it."

"You don't have to," he said. "It's gone out."

Then I felt a terrible sense of loss and I told him, and we both laughed; and we went through the Holy Sonnets again, decided to skip Newman, talked about Hopkins.

"Look," I said, "I did the right thing, perhaps, but for the wrong reasons; if I do it again, it will still be for the wrong reasons; that's building a house on sand."

"No, it isn't," he said. And failed to explicate his text.

I burbled on for a time, making what I increasingly felt were excuses. Suddenly he broke in, "What are you doing here all alone?"

"Staying out of harm's way," I said. Too quickly. Knowing how dead were the roses on Mac Moan's road.

"That's a pretty poor reason for an existence."

"What do you think the Eglantines were doing but that? And a bit of embroidery?"

"They performed the rituals; they prayed."

"I can do that here."

"You don't."

"Look, Anthony, to lead a harmless existence in the twentieth century is a great accomplishment."

"Then the Eglantines were a great accomplishment."

I was trapped. I should never even have tried philosophy.

"I don't have enough faith, Anthony. I don't have enough belief . . . enough will, even, to try to please God."

He didn't answer that. He got out the account books of the Order.

I was fascinated. I had never seen the major ledgers, though I had, of course, kept records of our spending when I was in charge. I was surprised to find that the Order was as quietly rich as the city of London, Ont., itself: there were a great many bonds and city debentures, and large pieces of the Canadian Pacific Railways and Bell Canada; solid investments in insurance companies; secured deposits in trust companies. No relatives had claimed Mary Beatrice's large dowry, and Mary Cicely had indeed had money, poor soul: her parents had been prosperous farmers when they died. A number of childless widows had thought Eglantine House the correct beneficiary of their husbands' over-strivings; if Eglantine House was a human dead end, a repository for women no one could think of what to do with, it was also a financial last resting place for a good many estates. From the dates of the investments it was easy to see that while Philip had been thinking of winding up the Order when I first met him, he had taken the opportunity of consolidating its portfolio on good advice. I need never have gone out to work at all, I thought with a pang; then smiled at the wisdom of Mary Rose, who kept me busy.

"Mary Elzevir?" I asked.

Anthony opened a leather satchel that was a cross between a book bag and a briefcase and brought out a stack of exercise books stuck together with an elastic; "Read, mark, learn and inwardly digest," he said.

"Later."

"Of course. You were the one who took out the medical insurance: she's well taken care of."

"Asher always said I couldn't manage money."

"I met Asher."

"Oh?" Small o.

"He thinks well of himself and ill of you."

"I'm not surprised."

"If I were you, my spiritual difficulty would be forgiving Asher."

"It's more complicated than that, Anthony: whenever I start to forgive Asher, I fall in love with him again."

"He's a prick."

The word sounded odd in the good brother's voice. I thought, it's myself I have to forgive, for drawing so many crooked pictures in my head. I wanted to ask him how he had met Asher and how Asher was and I asked myself if I wanted to hear that Asher was in a decline (with leprosy? That would have been grand) or that Asher was prospering (probably the truth and I hated it) and I decided finally that the statement I wanted was that Asher was a prick, and I let it go at that. If there's no absolute truth you might as well go for what you want.

"Look, Pelagia," Anthony said, "there's an establishment: Eglantine House exists. We need you to resurrect it; we are calling you; for practical reasons; and because we think you can do it."

To my amazement, I started to cry.

We were sitting on hard chairs at the kitchen table. Across from each other. I wanted Anthony to take my hands, I wanted him to comfort me. Then I realized that, within a framework of rules he accepted and I once had, he couldn't; and that was good, too: one could take no refuge in sentiment: one had to persevere.

"Asher says I can't go back to Ontario," I whispered. The final escape.

"He can't keep you out of Ontario. He doesn't have to support you if you return; that's all."

"Oh."

So we went back to the real subject, but not immediately. He put on his parka and went out for a walk and I made some kind of supper. After we ate, I went walking myself. We had come so close I didn't want to be alone with him any more; when I was tempted to ask if I could wear his parka, I knew how I felt about him and though I was glad I wasn't finished with sex, glad to feel my body still had desires and possibilities, I thought of things I might do and say and then of why I ought not to; I walked all the way up to the store in the cold and the wind and then twice around the gas pumps (Irving) because of course it was closed, and I came back somewhat cooler ready to argue again. But he had already gone into the livingroom for the night.

That was a strange, upset night; the wind came up again

and rattled the house in all its dimensions. I turned and groaned, moaned with the wind; shuddered as the snow blew like hail in the old, loose windowpanes. Half of me was wanting to putty them in the spring, as if I would ever get around to working with my hands in that male way, half of me was tied to the mast so I wouldn't rush in and throw myself on Anthony; I was trying to think and it wasn't thinking I was doing; I was drowned in an enormous surge of feeling: somebody wanted me; I wanted to be wanted; but I was used now to being wanted for bodily things, I was misinterpreting the signals all over the place, my self in rags and tatters floating around the house in eddies of wind, my old self lying on the hard dirty road listening to underground streams, my sensual self taunting Anthony, and another piece of me wrestling with all I could know of Hopkins' God, and me, who was I?

Awake until dawn; longing for one of the clouds of unknowing, Lord knows I had tried them all but cocaine. Longing for something, anything. Dr Stern's sleeping pills were at hand but somehow I thought, no, this is a good night, a valuable night, see it through; myself as a child in a fever and me bending over her, holding her forehead, cooling her body with Florida water, flailing, threshing the blankets with the violence of the wind. I was a child again, an open greedy mouth, a vessel of one ingredient only, longing: and it was not a man that would answer this time. (Oh, I could try, I thought. What would it matter? But it was like interfering with a happily married couple: there must be some ties unbroken if we are to survive; something is sacred, let it be him.) It struck me again as it had at the table that reaching out physically was irrelevant; that my hunger was not wholly physical any more than it was wholly spiritual, that what I wanted was not Anthony and not God, but something else.

A world.

I wanted a world; yes, that was it, and I wanted a world I could legislate, make my own; not own, not totally control, no, not that: ah, but that was it: have an importance in.

Pride, there, Pelagia.

Oh yes, pride and what if it's there and you can't help it you have to channel it, don't you? Put it in a place where it's useful.

Look, what else will I do, sit around and wait for the spring to come again, eat the world with my eyes, get thin, get fat, talk to the birds again, read all the books, good and bad, again, again, again; decide who is an anabaptist, who is a Manichean, which is the more Pelagian Pelagian? Name all the birds? Define the grasses? Count jellyfish? Make homes for stranded crabs? Leave footprints in snow in winter, sand in summer? For blizzard and tide? Is that the good life?

Before Anthony came I had said that that was so.

Then I was angry with him, truly angry. I wanted to go in and shake him, scream, "You spoiled my dream." Because he had; it wouldn't, again, be the same here. The simple acts I had taken pleasure in would be soiled because they hadn't met his measure. And I would be back again, back to not meeting someone's measure, puddling through a porridge of guilt and despair; the texture of the photography gritty and grainy, the colours of the grasses faded; I would see evil in the small stalked eyes of the crabs, in the smooth waddling forms of the scavenging birds only decay. Curse you, I cried in my heart, curse you, Brother Anthony. Asher has sent me, admittedly by mistake, to the one perfect place, and you have spoiled it.

Though I knew he hadn't.

Some of us hatch only in stages.

So I lay and cursed him, hated him, almost; emptied myself of feeling; wept for my field. Finally, slept. As the wind died.

It was late when I woke. He was reading at the table. He made me a cup of coffee and I sat up in bed and talked to him.

"I'm half in favour," I said, "for practical reasons."

"I prefer practical reasons," he said.

"I thought you might be more the type for prayer and fasting."

"Sometimes that's necessary, too. But I lack the gift for mysticism."

I forebore to tell him that the only time since I left the convent I had experienced anything close to a mystical vision I had

158

been in bed with a man I hardly knew. So I said I would come. And now I am here.

In the church I grew up in there were two varieties of call a minister could receive, as far as I know. One, from God, supplied his vocation; another, from a congregation, offered him a place in which to practise his mission. It seemed then, and seems to me now, a dubious practice to accept a call when one has no sure sense of vocation, but I have done so in obedience to my Bishop and, bitterly, for want of anything else to do.

And yet, and yet . . . I remain suspicious of doers. I still don't know whether I was right to give up my freedom, whether indeed a vision of action would have faded the colours of the shore and washed my footprints from the sand. I may have been very wrong to turn myself, practically, consciously, and hypocritically, back into Mary P. To leave what is called the world for the worldly-unworldly once again.

I read Mary Elzevir's journals: she had the true vision. She knew about God. The holocaust had burned Him into her soul.

I have this one night to turn the matter over and over again in my hands like a darning egg. What are my visions? What are my dreams: Can I fulfil them here? Are they any use to anyone else? Am I good enough to do good?

How I fed off the books in that house. How I have always nourished myself on them. Some week or other I curled myself up and read with astonishment and delight Cecil Woodham-Smith's life of Florence Nightingale. What interested me most was, of course, her relationship with her mother; what caught me up was the way she later despised ladies, particularly the religious ladies – both Catholic and Protestant nuns – she took with her to the Crimea (though some of the Sellonites were excused, if I remember). The need, she said, was not for soul-saving, but for life-saving. When men are dying in corridors running with filth, you get down on your knees and scrub, not pray; when governments have to be convinced, you collect statistics, not tears; when men are dying you apply bandages of sterile cotton, not of prayer.

I don't mean to compare myself with Nightingale; I have not

a jot of her ability or half her toughness; I wouldn't sag to the ground in fear if I met her, but I know what she meant and I agree. The religious life is a luxury in times of war.

And there is a war now and I finally accepted Philip's and Anthony's call to service not out of religious dedication but because, I suppose, I was brought up to believe that sensible people rolled up their sleeves and pitched into the war effort.

The fall-out from the battle of the sexes is getting worse every day and will continue to do so. The men are running scared but not scared enough to carry out my mad plan for holocaust as relief: but there is a ghastly woman-hate in the air and they are acting it out; and women are responding with either aggression or fear. Men, forced by politics and literature and the facts in front of their eyes to see women as they are, are frightened. It is not for nothing that the Quebecois have used the analogy of forced marriage to present their case for separation from Canada: marriage is changing, people are afraid of change, war has broken out.

That is how I force myself to see it now at any rate. It is easier to live by analogy, and if you find the right one you can forge it into a different reality, pack your trunks for war instead of a nunnery. It is easier to choose to be a Martha in a war.

And it is only possible to convince others to act for you if you have convinced yourself.

And only possible to say good-bye to the snow-filled field, its white stained blue and grey by wind and sky, its firs covered to the tips with madcap snowdrifts, its edges blurred so the line between land and sea is more ambiguous than ever, give it a brief last look through salt-stung eyes, if you are convinced there is another field.

I packed my trunks to go not to China or West China, but to Eglantine House. I let the stove go out, I looked at the field, I hove myself fast against the bitter wind into Macdonald's wife's brother's pick-up to go to the ferry to go to the train. If I had looked longer I should have turned into a pillar of salt.

And I was glad there was no more time to think about the past. Any of the pasts.

160

Asher didn't like me; in the end, it came down to that. He didn't like me, and he was afraid of my having any power, even domestic power. As long as I was occupied by my son, he felt safe from me; but when I was unprotected, he trapped me and tied me up again. He had to keep me well tamped down in the silo of his mind. He was afraid, not so much of me, as of the spectacle of women with power.

And I have met many women who have the same fear of men. I have it myself, now, and for good reason.

And the fear and distrust are killing us.

I am still unable to see what Asher fears and dislikes in me so. I am, to myself, myself and that only. An object. He must have put me on a shelf that loomed over him. He must have made me stand for something that could destroy him.

If Asher were the only man who felt this way, there would be no point in doing what I am now going to do; but there are hundreds and thousands of them, men who are afraid of giving women any power, any power at all; who must bind them and hurt them, retain them as superior servants only; probably to prevent what they fear is the female side of themselves from getting out of hand. Yes, I think that's it; certainly I am afraid of that part of myself that has not been legislated female: and I am afraid, now, deeply afraid, of men. I know what they can do to me.

Fortunately, I am not called upon to be a physician. I do not have to heal myself. I think, once, I wanted to become whole again, to learn to love a man again, but it is really too late. Biologically I have no function any more, I cannot breed. Therefore, if I had to do with a man, my function would be domestic only, for one person only. Therefore, for a limited time only, I am going to operate Eglantine House as a kind of hospice, a refuge from the war: an alternative to the plan of disposing of us all at thirty, which I must say wounded Anthony when I suggested it, and made me like him a good deal. ("But I would never have known my grandmother," he said.)

I am sister superior; the title a sop to my pride. The spiritual director of the house, however, will be the novice mistress, Sister Mary Frances, who is to come in a couple of weeks. I have promised to accept her direction, particularly in the matter of exorcising hatred and despair.

You see, given the fact that I am not dead, given the lifespan of the Hebers in general (as opposed to that of my parents and Kenny, which was shortened by adversity), I have a long time to live; and I must use the rest of my life. I will use some of it to treat, in practical ways, a few of the victims of this war.

I cannot accept the fact that it was women who brought all sin into this world; or that they are dirty; or that they are unequal, stupid, or apt to wear sin, like a bat, in their hair. In the early church they were not equal: busy, perhaps, otherwheres, but there were active women mentioned in the Epistles. Some other doctrine flung them into the mud, some false interpretation, some guilty dream. The dream that created Pelagia, perhaps.

I flounder again. I haven't got it straight. Well, I'm allowed to flounder. If I had no sins I could not pray to be forgiven. I'll try again.

Once I was a child; a lonely child who talked to animals in peoples' barns and listened instead of to the radio to the voices of underground streams. Who fled marriage on the grounds that it was dangerous; married and found it was so; removed herself (with a little help from the law) and went to live alone; where she was happy, though dark visions crept in at the edge of her field.

What were her dreams, then, her desires?

Oh, beauty and hope and a kind of cleanness . . . like the clean breath of cows, the crunch of those long root things Peacock ground in the mangle, the bite of winter air: oh, she wanted things to be unequivocal and sure.

She wanted to be certain. To know. To know not, as she thought, philosophy, but something more important. The truth. The truth for her. Not always to be torn, to wonder if. . . .

There is nothing uncertain about a rose, nothing tentative. Temporary, certainly, the flower: but not uncertain.

That's why I'm here. That's why I'm here.

We are going to run a women's hostel. Give me your tired, your poor, she says. No, I mustn't be cynical. The use that this house and its endowment can be put to is as a women's hostel run by a small staff of sisters with the help of Dr Margaret Charters, the psychiatrist. She will not take vows, and she shall be paid very well indeed, for she will need luxuries.

Anthony tested me by saying I should be novice mistress. I refused. I have forgotten the order of devotions; nones and tierce are mediaeval words to me, that is all. Sacramentalism barely interests me. My function is managerial. I shall be sister superior for a term of five years. Then we shall elect another head. That will be my time of trial. I find I love power as much as Asher did.

Philip has a long list of postulants: we have come in fashion again. I shall interview them carefully. I want women who will devote themselves entirely to the work, who know the world they have left and why they have left it. I won't have man-haters, I won't have those who still have lovers, even lesbian lovers: I want women whose interests are not divided. All of us must invest all of our whole selves in the house.

I shall examine my women's motives with great care, like the rabbi who must be approached three times. Who knows better than I do the ambivalence, the weak commitment produced by bad faith? (Though I must say I am prejudiced in favour of one would-be postulant who has had experience running a day nursery.)

I know what I want now; I am certain of this as I am of very few things. I want a core of women helping other women to put their lives (their souls we shall leave to Dr Margaret Charters and the novice mistress) in order. The casualties are coming in in greater and greater numbers, and though I would like to take the men, too, and bang all their heads together, and cry, "Off with the old, on with the new" and "You must love one another or die!" it is women I am committed to working with and I shall do that. If I can organize us efficiently, if we can do an eightieth of the work they do at Nellie's hostel in Toronto we can justify the faith that provided our income.

Heavens, I'm a practical Pelagian now. I've come out of my shell to do this work. Not for Philip's sake, who needs no more plumes in his episcopal bonnet, not for Anthony's either. I will do this work for the good of my own immortal soul; but I will do it also knowing that I came here out of a need, not to serve, but to belong.

Everything has changed since I left Eglantine House, the liturgy, the hymn book, the custom of wearing habits. Meaning has been substituted, to a degree, for ritual. So we are free to dress as we want, do what we want, smoke even. I shall feel awkward without a habit but I suspect I shall hang onto that part of my wardrobe which is navy blue, and we'll mostly all be happy enough to exchange our brassieres for Sister Bea's hand-made underwear and we'll probably ritualize ourselves automatically. I'd fancy it if we all wore T-shirts with anchors on them ("Will your anchor hold in the storms of life?" Not a hope, brother), but that's almost a literary conceit; we gave those up in the seventeenth century though word hadn't reached western Ontario until recently. Oh, I suppose we'll wear whatever sober garments we can find – go back to the old catalogue system we used for hats – and wear them to rags, until they're old and soft and enjoyable. I shall, anyhow.

Then we'll go out to women and say, if you need me, I'm here. They'll come. In a month, this house, this quiet, blessedly silent house will be a crawling mass of non-contemplative, cross, contentious humanity. Kids throwing stones at the chapel windows, drunken husbands beating obscenely on the door. We'll sort out the beaters from the beaten, the drunks from the health-food nuts, the masochists from the maoists. Scrub up the children, teach them not to fear. . . .

Oh Rita, Rita. . . .

Dr Pusey, I am ready.

I am standing in front of Heberville church belting out, "Fling out the Life-Line." I am the bloody-minded Martha that my mother was, Grammacrae was. God give me grace to taint my bloody-mindedness with love.

Well, we are what we are, aren't we? And if not what we once were, at least . . . grown up.

I was no good at being a Mary, and at least, as Philip said, meaning I know not what and do not wish to know, I've had "a world of experience." It will serve me. If we turn into a bunch of saffron-robed Buddhists it only means I've left enough doors open, I suppose.

Anthony was shocked when I told him how much sleep I wanted to include in the new Rule. Women need more, I said, thinking of broken nights and fatigue and the fact that there'll be prayer and fasting enough if we do real, not toy, social work. The really devoted ones will, like Mary Elzevir, evolve their own rituals. (Will they teach Marg Charters that there is a way of being happily mad, as Elzevir has taught me?) The others may use what words they want for what they do. They can say they are here for headspace and diet as long as they meditate in chapel and not in front of the television set. I don't want them to be so loose the new bishop (Philip is retiring in May) turns up looking like a frowning school inspector.

I talked to Anthony about Mary Rose and Sister Harriet Isbister to my heart's content. It was a relief from running through my case history with psychiatrists. We then branched out to monasticism in general and decided that it is probably born and bred puritans like ourselves who dream of living alone in holy mountains. We talked all one long night about Pelagius and Dionysus the Aereopagite.

When we talked about things as they are now I was very surprised. The degree of unbelief that is now permissible is astonishing. I can believe as little of the catechism and the Thirty-Nine Articles as I wish. Which is just as well.

So I am Mary Pelagia again. Sister Superior. As Sister Mary Rose indicated I ought to be in a last, flattering, and moving letter to Philip.

Little me? Who couldn't be trusted to dust old Mrs Bowen's Chinese pots?

Not little me: Sister Mary Pelagia.

Look, I said to Anthony, faith isn't something you put on and off like a habit. Faith is there and I don't have it any more.

You will, he said, if you believe in grace.

Finally I heard my voice rolling up its sleeves and I knew that

I was at the end of a long and delicious seduction. *Nor ever chaste except You. . . .*

I won't see my field when it comes back this summer. I won't see Mac Moan's road. I hope we can get a sister who's good with roses. Surely we don't have to give everything up. . . .

I don't know. I don't know. I'll never know. One day I'm sure my sanity lies on the seashore, another I want a lover, on the third I'm organizing a playground. I'm capable in one breath of dismissing union with the one as anti-intellectual claptrap invented to control the masses, in the next of repeating the Jesus Prayer twenty times. Hoping, too, that it's slid from head to heart like heavy water. Swearing, then quoting Hopkins. I tell Philip I won't confess to the likes of Father Brander, then when he produces a female I won't want to confess to her, either. I've confessed enough, I hear myself saying, all the time I was trying to be a miserable sinner, I was a miserable failure; the trouble is with me I'm too bloody good to be true.

Though I'm not.

Ah well, I guess there's nothing hypocritical in telling myself I'm starting a women's commune, and then trying to believe in it. I don't want to lose myself in the cloud of unknowing, just to believe enough in goodness to call it God. I told Philip that I won't take all that stuff about women bringing sin into the world and therefore having constantly to be beaten for it. I won't believe we're essentially better or essentially worse than men. Leave the virgins and the unicorns back in the middle ages, I'm living in the here and now.

"Fine," he said, with his lovely smile.

"I'm not good enough," I said almost sulkily.

"You will be."

I can't fight any longer. I'm tired. Tomorrow I've got to find people to help me put this house in shape. What do you call the kind of people who put in windows? Glaziers. Yes, I'll need glaziers. I need a cat as well. The mice are worse than they were in the country in the winter.

There must be somebody in London who makes good-looking wooden playground equipment. I don't want those ugly metal things spoiling Sister Harriet's cloister.

Enough. Enough. I've made my choice. I shall learn how to live with it. It's too late for a respectable Eglantine to be sitting up in the dark.

There's such a lot to do. Lord, will you allow us just a little garden in spite of the playground?

Funny. The chapel still smells of roses.

Marian Engel
The Tattooed Woman

Preface by Timothy Findley

Marian Engel insisted upon writing honestly and
fearlessly about the lives of women, and the stories in
The Tattooed Woman reflect her deepest concerns. The
reader is introduced to a wealth of wonderful, real
characters — women suffering, coping and often, but not
always, triumphing.

"The stories sparkle with humor yet touch depths of
pathos... Life is no rose garden. But Engel prefers
laughter to tears."
Patricia Morley The Ottawa Citizen

"Profound, compelling, exquisitely written, Engel's
fiction doesn't provide answers; rather, a sort of roadmap
of the emotions, it points to necessary alternative
directions."
Judith Fitzgerald
Kingston Whig Standard

"Engel was a great writer, one of the best, an often
fanciful chronicler of the heart's journey towards
self-knowledge."
Gerald Hill Edmonton Journal

Marian Engel
The Honeyman Festival
Introduction by Audrey Thomas

The Honeyman Festival chronicles one night in the life of
Minn Burge, a former starlet, now "nearer forty than
thirty" with three children and pregnant with a fourth.
Her journalist husband away on assignment, Minn
vaguely prepares for a party given in honour of
Honeyman, a movie director who was once her lover
in Paris.

From a wry and poignant perspective, Marian Engel
explores the dreams and nightmares of a woman caught
between a harried present and a faded but persistent
memory of a more glorious past.

"Marian Engel was one of her generation's most gifted
writers. Her piercing tales of love and loss demonstrate a
talent for illuminating the secret core of ordinary lives
with clear-sighted unsentimentality."
Ken Adachi The Toronto Star

"...one of the most graceful and humane writers in
contemporary Canadian fiction."
John Bemrose Maclean's

"Marian Engel's fiction...is clean and simple, implicative
and sonorous, illuminated by an artist's imaginative
power."
Doris Grumbach
The New York Times Book Review

"Engel is a treat. She makes comedy and sadness run
abreast...She entertains and informs in parallel, and is not
to be missed."
The Sunday Times

"Marian Engel's writing speaks of the wonder and love
and saving humour in the very midst of the muddle of
our lives...Hers was and continues to be a strong and
passionate voice."
Margaret Laurence Ethos